BOOKS BY DEAN HUGHES

Nutty for President

Honestly, Myron

Switching Tracks

*Millie Willenheimer and
the Chestnut Corporation*

*Nutty and
the Case of the Mastermind Thief*

Nutty and the Case of the Mastermind Thief

Nutty and the Case of the Mastermind Thief

Featuring William Bilks,
BOY GENIUS

by Dean Hughes

Atheneum 1985 New York

Library of Congress Cataloging in Publication Data

Hughes, Dean
Nutty and the mastermind thief.

SUMMARY: When Nutty investigates the disappearance
of the school Christmas fund from his locker, he and
his friends run into a bunch of thieves as well as a
more surprising solution.
1. Children's stories, American. [1. Schools—
Fiction. 2. Mystery and detective stories] I. Title.
PZ7.H87312Ns 1985   [Fic]   84-20486
ISBN 0-689-31094-3

Published simultaneously in Canada by
McClelland & Stewart, Ltd.
Composition by Heritage Press, Charlotte, North Carolina
Printed and bound by Fairfield Graphics, Fairfield, Pennsylvania
Designed by Mary Ahern
First Edition

Contents

Nutty and the Case of the Mastermind Thief

Chapter I

Nothing But Bills

"Nutty" Nutsell walked into the school cafeteria, and then he stopped. Maybe he wouldn't tell the other guys after all. They were going to think he was an idiot. But he needed help. And there were his friends —Bilbo and Orlando and Richie—all seated at their usual table.

"Hey, you guys," Nutty said as he walked up to them, "we have problems. *Big* problems. I have to talk to you right now."

"So talk," Bilbo said.

"Not here." Nutty was whispering now. "No one can hear this—except for you three. Come with me."

"Hold on a sec," Richie said. "Let me finish my lunch." He grinned, obviously aware that this would annoy Nutty.

"How can you eat that slop?" Nutty said.

But Orlando pointed his fork at Nutty and said,

"If I were you, Nutty, I wouldn't talk too much about that. You're the dude who got himself elected president by promising to get better lunches around here." Orlando was small and actually not very tough, but he liked to talk as though he were.

"I'm working on that, Orlando. It just takes a little while to . . . look, I don't have time to talk about that now. I've got to tell you what's happened."

Bilbo got up, slowly picked up his tray and said, "Come on, you guys—let's see what Nutty's done this time." The other two got up then, but all three went ahead and bussed their trays back to the kitchen, the way they were supposed to. This drove Nutty almost crazy. He was in the biggest mess of his life and his best friends were acting as if it were just any other day.

When the guys did come back, Nutty led them outside to the front lawn, to a place well away from the building and from other kids. Nutty was taller than the other three, but he bent forward a little and looked straight into their eyes.

"Listen, something really bad has happened. This morning I put that Christmas Fund money in my locker, and when I—"

"In your locker?" Bilbo said. "Criminy, Nutty, you were supposed to give that to Mrs. Ash after school yesterday."

4

Nutty had known Bilbo would say that. He suddenly felt sick. "I *know*, Bilbo. But when I went down to her classroom, she had already gone. She must have left early or something."

"Or you messed around too long and didn't get down there in time."

"Come on, Bilbo. Lay off." Nutty stood there for a second or two, looking down. "It's bad enough . . . anyway . . . I figured it wasn't that big of a deal. I just took the money home with me, and then I brought it back this morning."

"Oh, gees, Nutty," Orlando said, "you're not going to tell us that you lost it?"

"No, no. I brought it this morning. It was never out of my sight. But I got to school a little later than I should have, and so I had to head straight for class. I didn't want to be late."

"You *were* late."

"Not really—just a couple of—"

"But what did you do with the money?" Bilbo asked.

"Like I said, I put it in my locker. I didn't think—"

"Nutty, that was stupid," Richie said.

"Come on. What's so bad about that? I didn't think anything could happen to it if I just left it there until lunch." But they were all staring at him. Nutty

5

decided he *was* an idiot. He shook his head, and then he pushed back the shock of blond hair from his forehead.

"Are you saying that someone stole it?" Bilbo asked.

"Not all of it. Just the twenty-dollar bills. There were four of them."

The boys looked at him strangely, doubtfully. Nutty knew the story sounded stupid, but it was *true*. Someone really had taken eighty dollars and left the rest.

"Arc you sure, Nutty?" Orlando said. "Maybe it fell out of the sack or something."

"Orlando, I never even loosened the string on the sack. There's no way anything could have fallen out. The only thing I can figure is that someone knows my locker combination."

"How would anyone find that out?"

"I don't know, Orlando. But how else could it happen?"

And then Orlando started to laugh. Laugh! Nutty couldn't believe it.

"Oh, man," Orlando said, "you're turning out to be *some* president. When everyone finds out about this, all I can say is, you better leave town."

Nutty felt like punching Orlando—except that what he said was true. Everyone *would* be down on him. He could hear it all now: Stupid Nutty messed up again; he never should've been elected in the first place; he's still the same old goof-up he's always been.

"Look, Orlando, it's not my fault. If someone robbed me, I can't help that. If someone stuck you up with a gun, no one would put the blame on *you*."

"Sure, if everyone believed that's what happened. But we all know you, Nutty, and we know—"

"Wait a minute," Bilbo said, and he hesitated until the other guys looked at him. "Okay, Orlando, maybe people will say that. But I was with Nutty when we counted the money. And I saw him pull the drawstring tight and then loop it around and tie it. I know he shouldn't have put it in his locker, but I also know he didn't *lose* the money."

"Thanks, Bilbo," Nutty said.

"Don't thank me yet. I still don't see why you took it home. Why didn't you take it down to the office?"

"I was supposed to take it to Mrs. Ash."

"I know. But since she was gone, you could have given it to Dr. Dunlop's secretary."

Nutty knew that was right. In fact, he had almost taken it to the office; but the truth was, he hadn't wanted to run into Dr. Dunlop. Nutty had promised to bring in some suggested lunch menus, but he had never gotten around to doing them. So he just glanced at Bilbo and nodded his head. No point in even trying to explain.

"Look," Richie said, "the money is gone. That's the only thing that matters now. And I don't see what we can do about it."

"We've got to get it back somehow," Nutty said. "You're crazy if you think I'm going to announce to the whole school that I messed up. Orlando's right about what the kids would say."

"Oh, come on, Nutty. How are we supposed to get the money back?"

"I'm not sure. But I *do* think I know who took it."

"What are you talking about?" Bilbo said.

"Jim Hobble still hates me, right? He'd love to get back at me for beating him out in the election. And he'd love to make me look like a lousy president."

"He doesn't need to," Orlando said. "You're taking care of that yourself."

Nutty gave Orlando a dirty look, but Bilbo ignored the remark and said, "Come on, Nutty. Hobble's a jerk, but he's not the kind to do something like that."

"Maybe not," Nutty said. "But Rod Fowler is. And Hobble has been hanging around with Fowler a lot lately."

The boys seemed to consider that, but Bilbo said, "I don't know. I guess that's possible. But how could you ever prove it?"

"Well, there's more to it than that. His locker is just down from mine. He's probably had lots of chances to watch me work my combination."

"I'll tell you something else," Richie said. "I heard that Fowler got moved here to the lab school because he got in some kind of trouble over at Ridgeview."

"That doesn't prove anything," Bilbo said.

"Look, eighty bucks is a lot of money," Orlando said. "Just about anyone in the school might have taken it."

"But think about it, Orlando. We had almost three hundred dollars in that sack. If someone just wanted the money, why not take it all? It looks to me like someone was more interested in making me look bad. Who's going to believe that someone stole part of it and left the rest?"

All the boys nodded, which made Nutty feel a little better. At least he wouldn't have to face the whole thing by himself.

"Maybe . . ." Nutty said, but he was still working on an idea that hadn't come quite clear. "I think maybe I can stall Mrs. Ash for a little while. I'll have to tell her what happened, but maybe she'll give me a few days to try to get the rest back."

"What good will that do?" Richie said.

"I'm not exactly sure. I'm thinking we can try to set Hobble up somehow—and trap him."

"Trap him? What are you talking about?"

"I don't know exactly. I haven't gotten that far yet. I need to have you guys help me think of something." They all stood there looking at Nutty; and long before anyone said it, he knew what they were thinking. And so he said it himself: "Maybe we better call William Bilks."

Chapter II

Genius at Work

The boys met at Nutty's house that night. William was the last to arrive, and Nutty tried to whisk him off to the bedroom quickly so the meeting could begin. But William, as always, took his time removing his coat. Then he spotted Mr. and Mrs. Nutsell in the living room. He strutted in and shook hands with each of them, exchanging a few pleasantries.

Same old William. My grandpa doesn't act that old, Nutty thought to himself.

"Well, William," Dad was saying, "how do you like the private school they put you in? Do you miss the lab school?"

"Oh, no. It's worked out fine. And I've been taking a night class at the college. I enjoy that."

"A college course?" Mom said. "At ten years old? That must be quite a challenge."

"Well, no—not really. But then, I'll soon be eleven." He nodded, quite seriously, and then he did smile enough to show that he *was* joking. "The fact is, I have to occupy myself with various projects to keep life from getting dull. That's why I'm glad Nutty —or I guess you call him Freddie—has cooked up something for me. I'm anxious to see what it is."

Nutty about died. That's all he needed. Mom and Dad were curious enough without William spilling the beans. Nutty started urging William out of the room, with a hand on his back, but Dad stood up and said, "What's up, Freddie? You didn't tell us what your meeting is about. It sounds like high-level stuff."

"I'll talk to you about it later," Nutty said, and his "urging" turned into pushing.

When they reached the bedroom, and the door was shut, Nutty said, "William, I don't want my parents to know anything about this. So if they bring it up again, watch what you say."

"Well, all right. Excuse me. I'm really very sorry. Naturally I assumed you would talk to your parents about anything of importance. I discuss virtually everything with—"

"Well, I don't. Not *everything*. And this is something you can't mention to anyone. Not even *your* parents."

"Fine. Fine. You can trust me." William glanced

around at the other boys. Bilbo and Richie were sitting on Nutty's bed, and Orlando was sprawled out on the floor. William had to greet each one, and shake hands. He asked Bilbo if he was still reading Tolkien, and he queried Orlando about his response to the World Series. Nutty was getting more nervous every second. He wanted to get down to business.

"We're doing all right," Richie said, in answer to William. "It's your old buddy Nutty whose goose is in the cooker."

"Is that so?" William said. "Tell me what's been going on. Do you mind if I have a seat?"

Nutty motioned to the one chair in the room, and William sat down, his short legs barely touching the floor. "Let's put it this way," Orlando said. "Nutty *is* the goose. He's *already* cooked. He's just stalling a little before they slice him up and serve him for dinner."

"Sounds like things have gone afoul," William said, and he chuckled to himself. Only Bilbo laughed with him.

Nutty, too anxious to sit still for such fooling around, quickly began to spill out the whole story. William at once became quite serious, listening carefully, asking a few questions for clarification.

"What was Mrs. Ash's reaction to all this?" he said, after Nutty had finished.

"To tell you the truth, I'm not sure she believed

me. She took the money that was left, and I think she just assumed that I lost the rest. But she said she would give me until our Student Council meeting before she told the other kids. She kept hinting that I should cover the loss myself—or get my dad to."

"Would your father do that?"

"I don't know. But I don't want to ask him. He'd croak if he found out I was messing up as president. It means more to him than it does to me."

"Yeah, well, that's obvious," Orlando mumbled.

"When's the Student Council meeting?"

"I'm not sure. Friday, I think."

"Nutty," Orlando said, "you're the president. If you don't know, who does?"

"I *do* know. I'm pretty sure it's on Friday."

"That's three days," Bilbo said. "That's not much time."

"No it isn't." William seemed lost in his own thoughts for a moment, but then he said, "It's a very strange set of circumstances."

"But one thing Nutty didn't tell you," Bilbo said. "He thinks he knows who did it."

"Oh, really?" William looked at Nutty. "And who might that be?"

Nutty had never sat down, but now he moved closer to William and sat on the floor. "I think it was Hobble—along with his buddy, Rod Fowler." He explained his theory.

William listened intently again, and then he said, "Now that's certainly a possibility. The motive does make sense, and it does appear that someone knows your combination."

"So how do we catch them? Is there some way we could set something up and then trap them?"

"Let me give this some thought," William said, and he leaned back and sat quietly for some time, his brain computing away. Nutty was hoping like mad that something good would "print out" in the next few minutes. If William couldn't get to the bottom of things, no one could.

When William finally took his hand away from his chin, he only said, "Did you notice anything that could be a clue? Did you look over your locker *very* carefully?"

Nutty shrugged. "I guess not. I noticed that the drawstring on the sack was loose, so I grabbed it and looked inside. When I saw that the twenties were gone, I didn't think about checking around. Do you think I could have found something?"

"Well, one never knows, of course. It's not like these mystery stories you read, where there's always some little lead left behind. But on the other hand, if there was something, it would verify that we're on the right track."

"Let's go down and look," Orlando said, and he stood up.

"What are you talking about?" Richie said. "The school's been closed for hours."

"I know. But Mr. Skinner always leaves one of the back doors open, the one by the big garbage dumpster. I've gotten in that way a couple of times when I've left something at school that I needed."

"I guess I'm not the only one who forgets things," Nutty said, glaring at Orlando.

But William said, "As I recall, Skinner's a rather cranky sort. What would he think of our going in that way?"

"I don't know. He's never caught me," Orlando said, and he laughed.

"I think we'd be in big trouble," Bilbo said.

"Yes." William considered for a time. "On the other hand, we can't afford to lose a whole day. We need to have a look tonight. Nutty, do you have a flashlight?"

"My dad does. In the garage. But if we go walking out of here, my parents are going to start asking all kinds of questions."

"Yes. Yes, that is a problem. Supposing Bilbo and Orlando stayed here, continued to talk so that voices would be heard. You and I could go out the window. Can we get in the garage from the outside?"

"Yeah, but . . ."

"If you think not, that's fine with me. Perhaps it would be wiser to—"

"No, let's do it." Nutty couldn't stand the idea of waiting overnight before they started to do something. All the same, he knew he could be in a whole lot of trouble if he got caught sneaking in the school —or out his window. But William was already tugging at the window sash, and in another few seconds, Nutty was climbing out behind him.

Orlando had been right. The door at the school was open. William and Nutty stepped in slowly, let the door close behind them, and then waited. William had told Nutty to get inside and then to allow some time for their eyes to adjust to the dark. As it turned out, however, it was not as dark as they had expected. A light from down the hallway and around a corner made it possible for them to see fairly well.

"Okay," William whispered. "I don't hear Skinner, so there's no telling where he is. Let's move along close to the walls. If we see him, head back to this door, or to the front doors—whichever keeps him from seeing who we are."

Nutty nodded. He didn't dare speak. He'd have to shout to be heard over the sound of his beating heart.

But the boys made it down the hallway to the locker and still they heard nothing, saw nothing. The only problem now was that the light was too dim to see the numbers on the combination lock. "All right,"

17

William said, "give me the flashlight. I'll point to the lock, shield it all I can—and you get the locker open as fast as possible. Skinner would have to come from one end of the hall or the other. If he does, we run in the opposite direction. Okay?"

Nutty only nodded again, although he really wanted to run right then. The light came on, and for a moment he was blinded by it. When he finally tried to work the lock, he flubbed up twice before he got it right. The light seemed to be on forever. At last the locker came open, with a metallic twang.

William shut off the light, and they stood frozen for at least thirty seconds, before he said, "We're okay. He must not have heard us."

But Nutty still couldn't move. If he got caught, losing his position as president would only be the first thing that would happen to him.

"What good is this?" Nutty finally whispered. "We can't see anything."

"I know. I'll turn the light back on. You'll have to look rapidly."

"Look for what? The guy probably just grabbed the money and ran. What kind of clue would he leave?"

"But of course he didn't just grab and run, Nutty. He stopped, opened the bag, took out the twenties, decided to leave the rest."

"I know. That's weird. Why would he—"

"Just look, Nutty." The light came on. "I have reason to believe that something might be here."

Nutty was squinting, looking frantically about, feeling exposed again with that light on. But he saw nothing. His locker was in a mess, as usual, but everything seemed unchanged.

"Look on the shelf where the money was," William said.

Nutty stood on his toes. The only thing there was a slip of paper. He pulled it down and glanced at it, almost threw it back in the locker, and then realized that it was a note: "Nutty, you really ought—"

The light went out, and at the same time Nutty heard the sound. It was someone walking, something jingling—maybe keys. But which direction was it coming from?

"Back the way we came," William suddenly hissed. The two shot down the hall, Nutty nearly knocking William off his feet in the process. It felt good to be moving; and when he heard someone shout behind them, he only turned on more speed. They were out the back door and across the playground in a matter of seconds, and then they fell on their stomachs near some bushes by the back fence. Just seconds later they saw Skinner. He came out the door, looked around in all directions, then went back. As he went through the door, he was raising his keys to have a look at them. Obviously he intended to lock up.

William and Nutty didn't move for another minute, but then William said, "It's best that we get out of here quickly. He might call the police."

Nutty, just starting to relax, jumped up, and the two of them dashed for the gate in the fence. Once outside, they ran all the way back to Nutty's house.

"That didn't take long," Orlando said, as he helped Nutty through the window.

"Didn't it?" Nutty said. "I thought—"

But William was saying, "Let's see it, Nutty. What did the note say?"

The note was still wadded in Nutty's hand, but he hardly remembered he had it. He straightened it, and then read the carefully printed words. "Nutty, you really ought to be more careful. I could have taken your Nikes too—but they wouldn't fit me anyway."

Nutty looked up at William, and then around at the others. "That's weird," Orlando said. "Why would he be dumb enough to leave that?"

"Maybe he's not dumb," William said. "Maybe he's smart. Maybe he's even too smart for his own good."

"Not if we're talking about Hobble and Fowler. Those two don't have one good brain between the two of them."

William chuckled, and then he said, "Nutty, you better bring those athletic shoes home. I have a feeling this thief would like to have some more fun with you."

"The shoes *are* home. I brought them home today. I only left them there a couple of nights."

"Where are they? Let me have a look at them."

Nutty got them from his closet, and as he did, he said, "Orlando, you can't believe what you got us into. Old Skinner came around the corner, and we had to run like—"

"What size *are* they?" William said.

"I don't know. They must be—" Nutty had begun to open one of the shoes to have a look, but suddenly he let out a little yelp and dropped the shoe. A spider—a big brown one—rolled from the shoe. Nutty stomped on it, but by the time he did he knew that it was already dead. "How did *that* get in there?" he said.

"Probably just crawled in and died from the smell," Orlando suggested.

But William took the question seriously. "Maybe it did just crawl in. But there is also a chance that it was placed there on purpose."

Chapter III

The Plan

Nutty sat down on his bed. He was trying to make sense of all this. "William, I don't get it. Why wouldn't the guy just take my shoes? Why would he leave a note?"

"Well, logically, it makes no sense at all. And yet, I have a feeling he's enjoying himself a good deal at your expense. Leaving a note is a way to taunt you, and warning you about the shoes is a way of keeping you worried about what he might do in the future."

"Maybe he just wanted to teach Nutty a lesson," Bilbo said.

"That's a possibility, Bilbo. But I have the feeling this person won't be able to resist striking again, especially if he gets no reaction from his first attempt. And this time we'll be ready."

"*All right,*" Orlando said. "Let's set a trap: a

rope or a net or something that drops down on him when he opens the door."

"Please, please, Orlando. That's a little extreme, wouldn't you say? We don't want to go to jail for hanging someone."

"Well, what can we do then?"

"For now, I think we should go with something quite simple. Don't say *anything* tomorrow. If we're right—if the thief mainly wants to make Nutty look bad—and nothing happens, I don't think he'll be able to resist trying something else. If you fellows act as though everything is normal, he may think Nutty didn't see the note, and he may go for the shoes or try to leave another note."

"So what if he does?" Richie asked. "How does that help us?"

"We'll be watching. One of us must watch Nutty's locker every second of the day tomorrow, even if it means someone staying at the school tomorrow evening."

"William," Nutty said, "I don't see how we can do that."

"Can't one of you—"

"I can watch most of the day," Bilbo said. "If I slide my desk back just a little, I can see out the door —and I'm looking straight at the lockers. I'll just have to make sure the door stays open."

"What about lunch and recess?" Orlando said.

"Lunch is no problem," Nutty said. "And I can sneak back in during recess. Mrs. Smiley doesn't pay much attention to what we're doing."

"I can hang around for a while after school," Orlando said, "but I don't know if that will do any good. If the crook sees us around all the time, he won't do anything anyway."

William nodded solemnly, as though he had already thought of that. "You'll have to watch from a distance, and you'll have to be subtle. Bilbo can watch out of the corner of his eye; but Nutty and Orlando, you'll have to find some hiding place. Is there some spot along the hallway that you can watch from and not be seen?"

"What about the custodian's closet?" Nutty said. "It's just down the hall. Mr. Skinner leaves it unlocked. We could get in there and pull the door almost shut—just leave a crack to look through."

"Until Mr. Skinner comes along," Richie said.

"If he does, maybe I could just step out and say I was looking for a mop. I could make up something about somebody barfing in the cafeteria, or getting a nosebleed. I could make a big deal about being Student Council President and wanting to do my part by cleaning up."

"I hope you do it, too," Orlando said. "That would be your greatest accomplishment as president."

Nutty slugged Orlando on the shoulder, but William ignored all this. "I would be careful with that sort of thing, Nutty. He might check out your story and catch you in a lie. And not only that—I'm not sure what he saw tonight. He may have only heard us, but he might have seen our silhouettes. He may already have some idea of who it was."

Nutty didn't like the sound of that at all. He felt a little chill run along his neck. "What can we do then?"

"Isn't there anywhere else you could hide?"

"There's the boys' restroom, but guys might be coming in there for a while after school, and they would want to know what the heck we were doing."

"Well, all right. But watch for Skinner from a distance, and maybe get out before he notices what door you're coming from."

"I don't know about all this," Bilbo said. "Watching from the room is one thing, but hiding in closets, or sneaking into the school, that's something else. We could get ourselves in a lot of trouble."

"Well, it's up to you fellows," William said, very calmly. "Is it worth the chance?"

"I don't think it is."

"That's easy for you to say, Bilbo," Nutty said. "But if I don't get that money back by Friday, it's my chicken that's going to get plucked. I say we do whatever we can to catch those guys. And I still think it's

25

Hobble and Fowler. That dumb note sounds like something they would come up with."

"I'm not scared," Orlando said. "I'll hide in the closet."

"I didn't say I was scared. I just think—"

"We'll use wisdom, Bilbo," William said. "And right now that means breaking up this meeting before Nutty's parents wonder what's taking us so long."

"Yeah, that's right," Nutty said. "If they ask you anything on the way out, just say that we're doing some long-range planning. That's sort of true. And Dad will like the sound of it. He's worried I'm not being a good president." Nutty turned toward Orlando. "And none of *your* remarks."

But Orlando was looking at the door. Mr. Nutsell was just opening it; he poked his head in. "Freddie," he said, "come out here for a moment. Someone wants to talk to you."

Nutty didn't like the sound of this. He saw the concern in his dad's face. All the same, he walked out of his bedroom, and the other boys followed. And when Nutty came around the corner from the hall, he was looking straight at two policemen, in uniform, standing just inside the front door. For a moment his impulse was to take off running again.

"Freddie," Dad was saying, "these officers said that a couple of boys were seen in the school tonight.

The janitor said one of them looked like you." There was a pause, and Nutty was about to tell all, when Mr. Nutsell added. "I told them you've been here the whole evening."

"They weren't where you could see them the whole time, were they, sir?" one of the policemen asked.

"Well, no. But I've heard the sound of their voices the whole time. They never left. I can vouch for that."

"Well, that's fine. Mr. Skinner wasn't sure. I guess he chased a couple of kids out, and he got a look at one that was tall and thin. He knew your boy and said it could have been him."

Dad laughed. "Well, that's not very likely, officer. My son's the Student Council President."

"Oh, is that right? Well, I didn't know that. But then, there's nothing to say that the kids were into anything. Sometimes kids just come back to the school to get something they left. Skinner said he couldn't find anything missing, or anything wrong. He just gets concerned. He said he's had trouble lately with kids hanging around. If the boys hadn't taken off running, he probably wouldn't have made a big deal out of it."

The policeman really didn't seem too concerned. He was an older man with a graying mustache and a rather tired look in his eyes. But his partner, a younger man, was watching Nutty closely, and he sounded a little less trusting when he spoke. "So what *have* you boys been up to tonight?"

"We were having a planning meeting," Nutty said. "You know, talking about things I can get done as president." That was sort of true, Nutty told himself, but he knew that the guy was seeing right through him.

"And you didn't leave at all?"

Nutty took a breath. He knew the guilt would be thick in his voice if he lied. He couldn't do it.

But the older officer turned around. "If his father vouches for him, that's good enough," he said, and he turned back and smiled at Mr. Nutsell. He may not have been so sure either, but he wasn't about to insult anyone.

The younger policeman let that stand, but he said, "Do you know anyone else who is tall and slender—like you?"

"Jim Hobble is probably the tallest boy at the lab school," Bilbo said in quite a casual voice.

"Now that's interesting you say that," the older policeman said. "That's another name Mr. Skinner mentioned. In fact, he said the Hobble boy has been hanging around the building after school longer than he needs to. Do you boys know anything about that?"

"No," Nutty said. "I didn't know that."

"Well, all right. Thanks for your time. Sorry to bother you. You're the kind of boys we don't have to worry about. That's easy to see."

Nutty thanked him, and the two policemen left. Mr. Nutsell shut the door behind them and then said, "I'm sure glad I knew where you boys were tonight."

"Well, let me be honest with you, Mr. Nutsell," William said. Nutty felt his knees weaken. "We may not *always* be exactly where we're supposed to be, but we would never go down to the school and do something wrong. I can promise you that."

"Oh, believe me, I know that, William. I'm proud as I can be of Freddie. He's come a long way this year. And I think I have you boys to thank for much of that. You've been a good influence on him."

Nutty went to the closet and got William's coat. He could feel the heat in his face, and he didn't want his dad to have a good look at him.

But when he handed William's coat to him, William whispered, "Did you hear what the policeman said about Hobble?"

Nutty shot a look back at his dad, but Mr. Nutsell hadn't heard, or didn't show that he had. Nutty said, "Yeah." But he really didn't give it much thought until everyone was gone and he was back in his bedroom. Jim Hobble had been hanging around

29

after school. That didn't prove anything, but it fit. It was another piece in the puzzle. But they had to start finding a lot more pieces—and a whole lot faster. "If we don't, I'm a dead duck," Nutty said out loud.

Chapter IV

The
Boa Constrictor

The next day everyone watched the locker—and absolutely nothing happened. It was a long, worrisome day for Nutty. Right after school all the boys met at Nutty's locker, except for William.

"Look, you guys," Nutty told the others, "Orlando and I will wait for a chance, and then we'll slip into the closet. I've got an idea that now, once the halls have cleared out, will be the time when Hobble or Fowler will try to do something."

"How long are you going to stay in there?" Richie asked.

"Well, I'm not sure. Maybe a couple of hours. We'll have to watch for Mr. Skinner. I don't know how much he uses the stuff in this closet. If he comes along right away, we might have to get out and come

31

up with a new plan. Why don't you guys just go home, and I'll call if we need your help. If nothing happens, we'll probably need to hold another meeting."

"Well, all right," Richie said, "but if you want, I can come back and take over the watch after a while."

Nutty thought about that for a second, but Bilbo said, "I don't think that's a good idea. With Skinner around, too much coming and going could be dangerous."

Nutty thought that over, and then he said, "Okay, I think that's right. But can you guys stay long enough to help us get in the closet without getting spotted?"

"Sure," Bilbo said. "Let's get over by the door. When we see the chance, you two jump in. Once everything's clear, we'll give you three knocks. Don't crack the door until you hear us do that."

"Sounds good," Orlando said. "I love this kind of stuff. It's like a spy movie." They were walking over to the closet.

Nutty gave Orlando a sarcastic smile. "Maybe to *you* it is," he said.

"All right, get in now," Bilbo said. "No one's looking this way."

There were very few kids left around, but Nutty took another look each way as he opened the door, and then he and Orlando slipped in and shut the door behind them.

"Hey, it's dark in here," Orlando said.

"What did you expect?" Nutty was whispering. "And don't talk so loud."

"Isn't there a light in here?"

"Probably. But we can't turn it on. If we do, Skinner might spot it—or the thief could."

"Well, let's at least find the switch—in case we need it sometime." Orlando started shuffling around, and Nutty could hear him rubbing his hands up and down the wall. Then he tried the other side of the door, bumping into Nutty in the process. Suddenly the light came on.

"Okay. You found it. Now turn it off."

"Just a minute. Let's see what's in here."

"There's nothing but—"

"Look, Nutty." Orlando had lifted the top off a big trash barrel. "This thing's empty. If we had to, we could get in there."

"Both of us?"

"Well, it would be a tight squeeze, but if we *had* to, we could probably do it."

"No thanks, Orlando. I'm not really interested in doing any tight squeezing with you. You're not my type."

"Well, I—"

But the three knocks came on the door. "You

guys," Bilbo whispered from outside. "We're leaving. You can crack the door in just a minute; but turn that stupid light off. I can see it coming out the crack under the door."

Nutty flipped the light off. "Okay," he whispered back to Bilbo, "go ahead." And then he and Orlando stood silently in the darkness for a minute or so before Nutty slowly opened the door, a little at a time.

"Look, Nutty, if you think I like the idea of hugging you, you're nuts. I—"

"Ssshhhhh," Nutty said, as he got the door open just enough to see down the hallway. He had a clear view of his locker. Now it was just a matter of waiting.

But the wait turned out to be long, and not very exciting. The two boys traded off on the watch every few minutes, and otherwise, it was just a matter of standing in the dark. Once in a while a couple of kids would walk by, or a teacher would stroll down the hall, but no one took so much as a good look at Nutty's locker. Nutty spotted Skinner once, at the other end of the hall. He was about to warn Orlando when Skinner turned and went around the corner to another part of the building.

Orlando finally found himself a box to sit on and began to complain in a loud whisper. "Nutty, turn on the light and see if I'm asleep, will you? I can't tell anymore."

"Orlando, just keep still, will you?"

He did sit still for another minute or two, but then he said, "Look, Nutty, I think I'll take off. You can handle this by yourself, can't you?"

"Yeah, sure I can. That's probably a good idea anyway."

"What's the matter? Don't you like my work? How come you're trying to get rid of me?"

Nutty shook his head in the darkness, but he didn't say anything.

"No, really. I don't think anybody's coming, Nutty. Why don't we both take off?"

"I'm going to stay for a while. But you go ahead. Right now is a good time. There's no one in the hall."

"What's the matter—don't you like me?"

"Orlando, for crying out loud, would you lay off? This is serious stuff, whether you think so or not."

"Sure, you just want the trash barrel to yourself, that's all."

Nutty was starting to laugh, in spite of himself, and that made him mad. He turned around and shot out a little jab at Orlando. "Would you get out of here?" he said.

"Okay, okay." Orlando's laugh was entirely too loud.

"Wait a minute," Nutty said. "Now don't go out until I check and make sure . . . oh-oh."

"What's wrong."

"Here comes Skinner."

"Just walk out. Quick."

"It's too late. He'll see where we came from. Wait a minute. He's stopping." He watched to see what Skinner would do, his heart pounding and his breath stopping altogether.

"What's he doing?"

"I'm not sure. He's looking at a locker, I think."

"Yours?"

"No. It's farther down the hall. Hey—he's opening it up."

"Wow, Nutty. Maybe we caught the thief. Maybe old Skinner's been ripping kids off."

"Gees, Orlando, don't be stupid."

"Well, why not? He could—"

"Shush. Look, maybe we better make a break for it now." Nutty started to open the door, but at that moment Mr. Skinner shut the locker and turned in his direction. "Oh, no," Nutty said, "here he comes."

"The trash barrel," Orlando whispered, and now there was no humor left in his voice.

But Nutty was still watching. "Maybe he won't come clear down here. Maybe he's just going to . . .

no, he's angling this way. Jump in Orlando. Hurry. Nutty pulled the door closed; they were in the dark. Orlando seemed to take forever getting into the barrel. Nutty couldn't stand it. He started in and bumped hard against Orlando's shoulder. One of Nutty's feet slid down Orlando's chest. "Wait a sec," Orlando gasped, trying to push himself back and out of the way.

"Gees, let me in," Nutty said, frantic. The door would open any instant. Finally he was down next to Orlando, but when they both tried to crouch at the same time, their legs rammed against each other and neither one got anywhere. So Nutty grabbed Orlando by the shoulders and shoved him down, then forced himself into what space was left—in and around and over Orlando. Orlando grunted, but held his tongue.

The lid was still up! Nutty grabbed for it and missed, then grabbed again. He brought it down too hard, when he did get hold of it, and clunked himself on the head. With one last effort he squashed himself tighter against Orlando and felt the lid settle into place.

A second went by, maybe two. Then the door opened. Skinner came in, and Nutty heard him rustling about, moving things on shelves, and then mumbling to himself in his usual grouchy voice. Nutty didn't even take a breath, and he could tell that Orlando was doing the same. But then there was a clinking sound on the top of the barrel, and Nutty knew it was all over. The lid would come up any second.

But the light clicked off—Nutty heard the sound of it—and then the closet door closed; silence followed. Three or four seconds went by; neither boy moved. Then Orlando whispered, "Well, get off me, stupid. He's gone,"

Nutty did lift himself upward, just a little, but there was a problem. "Just a minute, Orlando," he said. "I think he set something on top of the barrel. I can't get up too fast."

Nutty was pushing upward, mainly with his head against the lid, but the lid was very heavy.

"Come on, Nutty, you're killing me. Just stand up."

"I can't yet. I'm trying to—"

"I swear, you've got to be a boa constrictor—or else you have ten legs. You're wrapped all around me."

"Shut up, Orlando. I can't open the lid any further. Whatever's on it is going to fall off and make a big noise."

"What are you talking about? We can't stay in here. My ribs will cave in."

Nutty knew that Orlando was only complaining to complain. Most of Nutty's weight was off him. But he was right; they couldn't stay in the barrel. Yet how were they going to get out? He reached around the lid now, trying to get hold of whatever was up there. His hand struck something like a wire, or a . . . *Bonk!* Something hit the lid. It was metal on metal, and it made a resounding noise.

And then something grabbed hold of Nutty's shoulder. He gasped and stood straight up. A horrible clanking noise followed, and then silence. Nutty had no idea what was going on—or what was in the closet with him—but he clambered out of the trash barrel, stepping all over Orlando in the process.

"Hey, watch it," Orlando mumbled. "Hey, that's my head. Take it easy."

But Nutty was out now, and he grabbed for the switch and threw on the light. There was nothing there. Nutty looked all about, still trying to think what had grabbed him by the shoulder. But now Orlando was standing up, and for some reason his hair was all matted and wet, and his shirt was wet besides.

"What happened?" Nutty said.

"You dumped water on me, you jerk," Orlando said.

"Water?"

"Yeah. What do you think's on *your* shirt?"

Nutty looked at his shoulder. It was wet. That's what he had felt. And now he saw the bucket on the floor. What he had grabbed was the handle of a bucket, full of water. It had turned over on the lid, and the water had run down on the two of them.

Suddenly Nutty spun around and switched the light off again; then he cracked the door. He couldn't see anyone. "Come on, Orlando. He didn't hear us. Let's get out of here while we can."

Orlando, for once, had nothing to say; he just climbed out of the barrel while Nutty took another look. Nutty took one step out the door, took a look around, and then said, "Okay, Orlando, let's go."

They hurried down the hallway, trying just to walk but coming closer to running. And then there was a sound behind them, maybe a door opening. "Hey," they heard from behind them, "what do you boys think you're doing?"

They stopped, frozen in place.

Chapter V

Skinned

Nutty and Orlando turned around. "Hello, Mr. Skinner," Orlando said. "How are you tonight?" Nutty was glad that Orlando could speak. His own mouth would not move.

Skinner was coming up the hallway toward them. He had apparently been in a classroom, or maybe a restroom, and had come out just in time to spot them. "What are you boys doing in here?"

"Uh . . . Nutty needed to get something out of his locker."

"But I locked the doors half an hour ago—*all* the doors. Now what did you boys do to get past them?"

"Oh," Orlando said, and then nothing more came out.

"One door wasn't quite shut, Mr. Skinner,"

Nutty said. "You must not have pulled it closed all the way."

"I pulled on every one of them doors. So don't give me that."

Nutty stood there, breathless, waiting for something to occur to him.

"Maybe some kid—or a teacher—was still inside," Orlando said. "Maybe someone went out after you locked up and didn't pull the door shut. Or maybe the wind—"

"Now look, I'm not having any more of this. Just what's so important that makes you come back here every night?" He had walked a little closer now, and Nutty knew that he had to notice how wet they were.

"Every night? This is the first time—"

"I'm pretty sure it was you two last night. I want to know what's going on. If something turns up missing around here, you two are going to be in very big trouble."

"Oh, no. We haven't done anything wrong. You see, I'm the Student Council President, and I have to—"

"*You* are?"

"Yes, sir."

"Are you sure?"

"Yeah, he is," Orlando said.

"Aren't you the Nutsell kid? The one who set

off the firecracker in the boys' room last year and caused me all that trouble?"

"Well, sir, that was an accident. I didn't know it would go off under water. I was actually trying to put it out."

"Maybe you should have tried *not lighting* it in the first place."

"Well, what happened was—"

"Look, never mind. Go to your locker. Get what you need and get out of here. And this is the *very* last time."

Suddenly Nutty remembered that they had already passed his locker. He turned and slowly walked across the hall; then he said, "Oh, there it is back there." He glanced back at Mr. Skinner, who was shaking his head.

"Don't you even know where your locker is?"

"Oh, sure, I guess I just . . . didn't think."

"Well, now, that's nothing new." Nutty went on to his locker, hoping that Skinner would walk away. But no such luck. He followed them, and when Nutty stopped he said, "Now hurry up, and then get out of here. I'm going to be watching until the two of you are out of the building. What I really ought to do is call the cops. If I could prove for sure that it was you two in here last night, that's just what I would do, too."

Nutty tried his locker combination and got it

fouled up. This brought back memories. He glanced over at Mr. Skinner with a sheepish look on his face, and then he worked it again. This time the door came open. Nutty reached inside and grabbed an old notebook—the first thing his hand touched—and then he shut the locker again.

Just as he turned to walk away, however, Mr. Skinner said, "Have you been writing on your locker?"

"What?"

"What's on the door?"

Nutty looked back. There was a strange mark, shaped a little like a four-leaf clover. It seemed to have been written with chalk. When Nutty tried to rub it off, it faded but didn't wipe away entirely. "I didn't do that," he said. "Honest."

"Yeah, well, you never do anything, do you? Honest. But it's sure strange how things seem to happen wherever you happen to be at the time."

"I'll get some paper towels and clean it off if you want me to. I don't mind at all, Mr. Skinner. I didn't do it, but—"

"No, just get going. I got work to do."

The boys turned and started out. The way to the front doors led right past Mr. Skinner. Nutty thought they had made it and was just beginning to breathe a little easier when Skinner said, "Hey, are you two wet?"

"Wet?" Orlando said, with that "who me?" tone of his.

"Yes, what's that all over your shoulders?"

"That's the new look," Orlando said.

"The new *look*?"

"Yeah, the wet look. You wet your hair so that it looks all plastered down. See how mine is."

"And you wet your shirt, too?"

"I guess we got a little carried away."

Mr. Skinner gave Orlando a long look, a very dry one. Nutty knew he would never go for such a dumb story.

But all he said was, "Get out of here. You kids are going to drive me nuts someday." It sounded almost as if he might want to laugh. But Nutty didn't dare take time to think about that. All he wanted was his freedom. He and Orlando did some fast walking, and finally they got outside where they could breathe again.

"The *wet* look," Nutty said, as soon as the door was shut behind them. "Orlando, that was *stupid*."

"Well, I didn't hear you coming up with anything better."

"Anything would have been better than that."

"Like what?"

Nutty decided not to continue such a silly discussion, especially since he had no answer.

* * *

It was time for another meeting, an emergency meeting. Nutty knew that although he and Orlando had avoided disaster—maybe—they hadn't accomplished one thing. As soon as he could, he got on the phone and scheduled a meeting for six-thirty—except that William said he could not be there until six-forty. And of course, that is precisely when he showed up.

Nutty tried to get him directly to the bedroom, coat and all, but Mr. Nutsell called out from the living room, "William, nice to see you again. What are you fellows up to?"

"Up to?"

Mr. Nutsell got up and walked, newspaper in hand, over to the entrance where the boys were. "What's the big deal you fellows are working on?"

"Well, you better discuss that with your son. It's not my position to—"

"I'll talk to you about it later, Dad," Nutty said, and once again he "urged" William down the hall.

"For heaven's sake," William said, once they were in the bedroom, "that was quite impolite."

"You were going to give it all away, William."

"No, no. I was only referring him to you. I'll not say anything. But don't expect me to tell lies. There was a time when I might have, but I've been studying the works of Socrates and of—"

"Yeah, you leave me to tell them. Orlando and I had to tell some beauties today."

46

"That's your choice, Nutty. I don't condone it."
He turned toward the other boys. "Good evening,
fellows. How did things go today? Did you keep a
close watch on the locker?"

"Yeah," Orlando said, "but nothing happened."

"Nothing at all?"

"Well, one thing—maybe," Nutty said. "I don't
know for sure that it meant anything."

"Just a moment," William said. He removed his
coat and laid it neatly across the foot of Nutty's bed.
Then he took his seat, the one the boys had left for
him. Orlando and Richie were on the floor and Bilbo
was sitting on Nutty's bed. Nutty sat down next to
Bilbo.

"All right," William said. "Let's hear it."

Chapter VI

Meeting
of the Minds

"We watched all day," Nutty said. "I mean every minute. And nothing happened. No one went anywhere near my locker. But we found something written on the front. It was—"

"Gees, Nutty," Orlando said, "aren't you going to tell him about the trash barrel?"

"No, Orlando, I'm not. It has nothing to do with all this."

"Sure it does."

"Go ahead and tell me, Nutty," William said. He was leaning forward, his elbows on his knees.

So Nutty told him about the incident in the closet and about getting stopped by Skinner. But he was brief; he really didn't want to go into all this.

"Did you clean up the water?" William asked.

Nutty had known that would be the first question. "Heck, no," Orlando said. "We were just trying to get out of there as fast as we could."

"That's unfortunate. You should have mopped up."

"That's easy to say now, William. But when that water poured down on my shoulder, I thought someone had grabbed me. I was really spooked."

"Well, never mind. What's done is done. Wasn't there something else—about your locker—that you wanted to tell me?"

"We found a mark on it," Orlando said. "It looked like some kind of symbol. And someone had to have put it on there today."

"What sort of symbol?"

"It looked like four circles," Nutty said, "all touching each other."

"No, Nutty," Orlando said. "They weren't exactly circles. They were more like—"

"Draw it for me," William said, pulling a ballpoint pen from his shirt pocket.

Nutty got up, found a sheet of paper, and handed it to Orlando. "*You* draw it," he said.

What Orlando drew looked like this:

"Is that right?" William asked Nutty.

"Yeah. That's what I meant. The circles flattened out where they touched each other."

Orlando took a little bow and said, "Exactly as you see it in my drawing, gentlemen."

William looked around at the boys. "Was there any time at all when you were not watching the locker? Any of you?"

"I looked away sometimes when we were in the closet," Nutty said, "but not long enough for someone to draw something like that."

"What about the time when you were in the barrel?"

"Well, yeah. But Skinner was right there during that time."

"That's who did it," Orlando said. "We saw him doing some other strange stuff. I think he's the crook."

"Come on, Orlando," Nutty said "He didn't stop that long. Besides, he wouldn't do something like that anyway."

"Why not?" Orlando said. "We think the thief is someone who doesn't like you. And Skinner *definitely* doesn't like you." And then after a pause, he added, "Of course, if we consider everyone who doesn't like you, we'll be working on this forever."

"Orlando, please," William said, sounding impatient. He turned to Bilbo. "Were you able to watch the whole time you were in class?"

"Pretty much. I could see right out the door. I wasn't staring out there every minute, but if anyone would have walked up to the locker, I know I would have seen him. Not only that; we were all at Nutty's locker right after school. I'm pretty sure there was nothing written on it then."

William turned toward Nutty, looking very curious. "When you were in the closet, did you notice the mark then?"

"No. But we were down the hall, and the light was not the greatest. We didn't see it until we were right at the locker."

William leaned back in his chair, looking off, the wheels in his head obviously turning. "This mark," he finally said. "What does it mean?"

"Heck, William," Richie said, "you're the guy who's supposed to figure stuff like that out."

"But does anyone have any ideas? Is it something familiar to anyone?"

"It looks sort of like a four-leaf clover," Nutty said.

"It looks more like two letter B's—back to back," Bilbo said.

"Yes. Or even in all four directions. I see that."

"It could be a flower," Richie said.

There were other suggestions: a package tied tight with string, two number 8's, four zeroes. Orlando even said it looked like a bowling ball wearing a big bow tie.

Nutty told Orlando to stop kidding around, but William said, "No, that's all right. We're just brainstorming at this point. It's right to mention anything that comes to mind." But when no other ideas came out, he said, "Well, then—do you see any connection at all between this mark and a spider?"

"A spider might climb on a clover leaf."

"Yes, yes. Do you see any implication in that?"

Richie shrugged. "No. It was just a connection."

"The B's could stand for the insect," Bilbo said. "They have stingers, just like a spider. But I don't know what that would tell us."

"Maybe it's the two B's in Hobble," Nutty said.

William nodded. "Yes, that occurred to me. But why the spider?"

"Maybe that stands for Fowler. Because he's creepy." This was from Orlando.

William sat back. He patted his fingers on his knees and stared into space. "Well, our problems have not changed," he said after a time. "We're not much closer than we were yesterday."

"Oh, man," Nutty said, "my drumsticks are about to get chewed."

"Now, now. Things are not so bad. The thief is still playing games with us. And besides, I have a new little trick up my sleeve."

"What?" Nutty said.

"All right, let me explain. It's something I came on quite by accident, working with my chemistry set: a liquid that has no value—except that it leaves a purple stain when it contacts human skin."

Everyone looked blank for a moment, and then Bilbo said, "You want to put some on the locker handle, right? And let the thief get some on his hands?"

"Exactly."

"Wait a minute," Nutty said. "That's not going to work. The guy will just see the stuff and not touch the handle."

"Ah—but that is the charm of the chemical. The liquid itself is clear. It reacts and turns purple only after it gets on someone's skin. Believe me, I learned that by experience."

"But won't he just scrub it off his hands?"

"Well, he may try, Nutty. But it only comes off with time. It gets into the pores, like printer's ink, and it takes more than scrubbing to get it off. Not only that, it takes a little while before the full color comes out. The thief may not even realize where it came from."

"Now we're talking," Orlando said. "That's a whole lot better than sitting around in a stupid closet with Nutty. All we'll have to do is spot the dude with the purple hands—and we got him."

"Except," William pronounced, and he paused until everyone looked at him. "We need to make certain that he has some reason to open the door—not just mark the outside again."

"How can we do that?" Richie said.

"We drop a hint. We say something around Hobble and Fowler to indicate that there is something valuable in the locker again. We may find that they are not the culprits after all, but for now we still must treat them as the prime suspects."

"I can do it," Orlando said.

"Do what?"

"Say something to those guys. I'll just—"

"I'm sorry, Orlando, but we need someone with a little more sense of subtlety. No offense intended. But I think Richie might be a better choice."

Richie nodded. "What should I say?"

"That's easy," Orlando said. "Just say, real casual like, 'Hey, in case you two jerks are wondering, there's still more loot to rip off in Nutty's locker.'"

William smiled, but Nutty didn't think it was funny. Nothing seemed funny to him any more.

"William," Bilbo said, "aren't you putting too much stress on Hobble and Fowler? I don't think those two are smart enough to do something like this. It takes more of a brainy type to get a bang out of matching wits with you."

William nodded, and he looked at Bilbo thoughtfully. "Someone who likes to think of himself as something of an intellectual—or even a mastermind?"

"Well, not necessarily. But at least someone who would enjoy thinking up clues and watching us struggle."

Again William nodded. "I agree, Bilbo," he said. "I think you are quite right. But I'm just setting a trap. Any mouse that wants to wander in is welcome. And remember, a trap may not always be as simple as it first appears."

Chapter VII

The Vanishing Clue

When the boys went to lunch the next day, Richie was the last to come in. He gave Nutty a little nod, and he looked rather pleased.

"Did you take care of it?" Nutty asked.

"Yeah. Just now."

"What did you say?" Orlando wanted to know.

Richie glanced toward the door and then quickly around the room. "All I had to do was walk by them, and they started calling me 'Nutty's Buddy,' the way they always do. I just let 'em talk until Fowler said something about Nutty not keeping any of his campaign promises. So I just said, 'Yeah, well, Nutty probably never will do any of that stuff.' "

"Hey, thanks a lot."

"Look, I was trying to get them to listen to me. And it worked. Right off, Hobble said something about how stupid you are."

"*Stupid*? That jerk. I ought to go knock his head off."

"Just listen, will you?" Richie shook his head in disgust. "I said, 'Ah, I don't know. Nutty's not really stupid. He just doesn't think sometimes. I guess you heard about him leaving that money in his locker.'"

"What did they look like?" Nutty asked. "Could you tell they knew what you were talking about?"

Richie thought about that. "Actually, they handled it pretty well. Hobble just said, 'What money?'"

"What did you tell them?" Bilbo asked. "You didn't get too obvious did you?"

"No. I just said, 'Well, never mind. I shouldn't have said anything. But to tell you the truth, I don't think Nutty will ever learn. This morning he went right back to his locker, and you wouldn't believe what he put—' And then I stopped, and I said, 'Well, I better not say what it was.'"

Nutty was holding a sandwich halfway to his mouth—one he had brought from home. "Gee, I don't know, Richie. That might have been too direct. Do you really think they went for it?"

"I think so. At least they seemed to."

Orlando said, "Did they get that look in their

eyes like guilty guys do on TV?" He pulled his head down close to his shoulders and shifted his eyes back and forth.

"No, Orlando, they're not *that* dumb. But they asked me a lot of questions about the money and what had happened."

"Look, here they come," Bilbo said. Nutty looked up to see them come strolling toward the table.

"Hey, Nutty," Hobble said, loudly and from some distance, "what have you messed up so far today?"

Nutty waited until Hobble got closer, and then he said, "It's sure nice to see you, Jim. I hope you're feeling well." He paused, and then he added, "I'm just fine, thank you."

Hobble stepped closer to the table, and so did Fowler. "I'm thinking *I'll* mess something up today," Hobble said. "Your *face*."

Nutty laughed. "The weather's been nice for this time of year, hasn't it? Do you think it will snow one of these days?"

"You're cute, Nutty. Really cute."

"Why, thank you, Jim. That's very nice of you to say so."

And Orlando added, "You're a nice-looking boy yourself, Jim."

This did not go over well. Hobble pointed his

finger at Nutty's face, almost touching his nose. "You're going to get it, Nutty. I'm not finished with you."

It was time to let the whole thing drop, but when Hobble started to strut away, Nutty couldn't resist one last shot. "Oh, Jim," he said, and Hobble stopped. "You're not supposed to break the school rules."

"What?"

"No pets at school, Jim. I see you have your little doggy following you around."

This did not go over well. Hobble fumed, and Fowler demanded that Nutty meet him outside right after school. Nutty just laughed, which only made things worse. When the two finally left, Orlando said, "Nutty, are you out of your mind?"

"Probably. But I want them good and mad at me. I want them to go after my locker again tonight. I want purple all over their hands the next time we see them."

"Yeah, well, some of the purple might get transferred to your nose."

Nutty knew that was true. But right how he was willing to take the chance.

That afternoon, right after school, all the boys gathered at Nutty's locker. They had watched carefully all day, but nothing had happened. As soon as the crowd in the hall thinned a little, Nutty took the chemical out of his locker, dabbed some of it on a cotton ball, and quickly wiped it all over the handle. For good measure, he wet the cotton a second time and put on another coat. The boys stood close around Nutty so that no one would see what he was doing. And then they left.

Nutty put in a long evening at home, wondering how everything would turn out. And it didn't help much to have his parents asking questions. At dinner Mr. Nutsell said, "Freddie what's all the hush-hush about your meetings?"

Nutty acted as if he needed to chew his food for a while, and he tried to think what to say. "There's no hush-hush, Dad. We just had a lot to do. I didn't want William to spend too much of our time chatting with you. You know how he is."

"So what are the meetings for then?"

"Well . . . school lunches, mainly." Nutty felt his cheeks get warm. He hated all the lying he had been doing the last few days.

"What is happening on those lunches?" Mrs. Nutsell asked.

"Dr. Dunlop wants me to submit some menus. He says he's willing to consider changes, but he wants specific menus to decide on. I think he's just stalling, but I'm trying to make him keep his word."

60

All that was true. But then Nutty added, "So we're working on some menus," and the heat in his cheeks spread to his ears.

Susie, Nutty's little sister, had not seemed to pay much attention until now. She was fiddling with her mixed vegetables, not really eating much. "Well, Nutty," she said without warning, "you better do something pretty soon. All the kids are starting to say they shouldn't have voted for you."

"Is that right?" Dad said, and he sounded concerned. "That hardly seems fair. A guy needs a little time to get certain things done."

"Not *that* long," Susie said.

"*Susie,*" Mom said. "I hope you stick up for your brother."

"Mainly, I try not to let anyone know he *is* my brother. But I'm afraid the word is out."

Nutty gave her a sarcastic little smile, but what she had said made him feel awful. And things didn't get any better when Dad started in on his good old speech about having "drive" and "stick-to-it" qualities. Worst of all, he said he would like to have a look at the menus.

Hot cheeks again—and burning ears. Nutty had to make up something about leaving the menus at school. "But I'll bring them home tomorrow, Dad. Maybe you can give me some advice."

Dad liked that. He even went off on a spiel about his days working in a restaurant when he was in college. That was all well and good, but now Nutty had to come up with some kind of menus that he could show his dad the next day. He ended up staying up rather late doing that and then having a little trouble getting up the next morning. He made it to school in time, but he had planned to get there early. He was going to check out his locker, and then, if there was any sign the locker had been opened, he would wait and watch for Hobble and Fowler to show up.

But when he got to school, Richie and Orlando were waiting out front. "Hurry," Orlando said. "We checked your locker, and someone's been messing around with the outside. The mark is changed. We need to look inside to see—"

He stopped and looked off behind Nutty. Nutty turned to see Hobble and Fowler coming up the walk. Hobble had that usual cocky look about him, but it was Fowler who said, "Hey, Nutty, where's your old Buddy Bilbo this morning? Is he feeling sick or something?"

Nutty was surprised. He had expected a challenge to fight. But what really interested him were Fowler's hands. Unfortunately, he couldn't see them. "Hey Fowler," he finally said, "what's that on your hands?"

"On my hands?" Fowler said. He turned toward Nutty and held his hands up. They were clean.

"No, I meant Hobble," Nutty said.

Hobble held up his hands, and they were clean too—or at least they weren't purple. Nutty felt like a real bird-brain.

"What are you talking about?" Hobble said.

"Nothing. What are you standing there looking at your hands for? You're a little strange, aren't you?"

Hobble didn't like that. He stepped up close to Nutty, almost on top if him. "Meet me right here after school, Nutty."

"No thanks. You're not my type."

Suddenly Hobble thrust both hands out and gave Nutty a shove. Nutty stumbled back but didn't fall. "I'm going to find you after school today, Nutty. I'm not taking any more of your cute stuff."

"You can try to hide," Fowler said, "but we have other ways of dealing with you."

"Shut up, Fowler," Hobble said, and then he looked at Nutty again. "Today. After school. That's a promise."

Nutty said nothing. He let them walk away.

"Nutty, he's going to kill you," Orlando said.

Nutty let out a long breath, and then he said, "Maybe so. But what happened? Why aren't their hands purple?"

"Maybe they just marked the outside. Maybe they didn't touch the handle," Richie said.

"Let's go look."

The three of them walked down the hall and stopped at Nutty's locker. The mark that had been there before was gone. It had been wiped away. And a new mark, a large circle, had taken its place. Just that: a big zero or letter O.

Nutty worked the combination and pulled open the door. Nothing seemed changed. The trap hadn't worked. They hadn't even opened the door.

Then Richie said, "Hey, what's this?"

It was another mark, inside the locker door, a little circle with a line through it—a line that extended on one side but not the other. It looked like a little dagger.

"They didn't take anything because there was nothing to take," Nutty said. "But they wanted me to know that they had opened the door."

"Maybe the chemical didn't work," Orlando said.

"It worked," Nutty said. He held up his hand. On his thumb was a deep purple mark, the size of a quarter. "I scrubbed like crazy last night, and it wouldn't come off."

The three of them were silent for several seconds. Nutty knew he was in big trouble. He didn't see how he was going to get that eighty dollars back before Friday.

"Those guys must be smarter than we thought," Richie said. Nutty had to agree.

Chapter VIII

Student Council

When Nutty walked into class, he found Bilbo already there sitting in his seat at the back of the room. "Gees, Bilbo," he said, "you aren't going to believe what—"

But someone was tapping him on the back. Nutty turned around and saw that it was Angela Vanghent. "Nutty," she said, "I've got to hurry to get to class, but I was just wondering what we're doing in Student Council today."

"Today? It's not today. It's tomorrow."

"No, Nutty. It's today. I hope you haven't forgotten—"

"No—I haven't. I was just kidding." But Nutty was suddenly not feeling very well. "I know it's today."

Angela didn't seem quite sure she believed him.

She said, rather hesitantly, "Well, then, what do you plan to do?"

"Well . . ." Nutty was thinking hard. "Maybe we better talk about . . . school lunches. I've been working on those menus that Dunlop wants. And maybe we could talk about the skiing trip we discussed last time."

"Have you done any work on that?"

"Yeah. Sort of. A little."

"Well, okay. And we do need to decide exactly how we're going to use the Christmas money."

"Yeah. That, too." Nutty felt sure he was turning red—or maybe white. Angela hurried off, and Nutty turned around and looked at Bilbo. But Bilbo wasn't even looking at him. Nutty was sort of relieved. He needed time to think.

He went to his desk and sat down. "This will work out," he told himself. "It's all sort of funny if you look at it the right way. I only seem to be a dead duck. A dying swan. A clay pigeon. A pheasant under glass. Sure my problems have come home to roost, but with a little nest egg I'll be flying high."

Or maybe there wasn't a funny side to it.

All that day Nutty debated with himself about what he could do. Mrs. Ash was his only hope, and so he went to her room just as soon as school was out. But she wouldn't budge this time. She said the other kids had to know. In a way, that was a relief. Nutty decided it was time to give up and face the music. "But will you let *me* tell them?" he said, and she did agree to that.

Nutty felt he could explain the situation better than Mrs. Ash would. At least he believed his own story. But by the time he called the meeting to order, he was nothing but nerve endings. There were a couple of kids missing, and he asked about them, but he really didn't listen to the excuses that were offered.

He was about to go ahead with his confession—get it over first—when Jerry Robinson, a kid in the sixth grade, said, "Aren't you going to have the minutes read?"

"Oh yeah. Go ahead."

"I'm not the secretary. Larry is."

"I know. That's what I meant. Larry, go ahead."

But once again, Nutty didn't listen. He knew what everyone was going to think of him as soon as he admitted what had happened. He wondered how many votes they had to have to kick him out of office. His dad would die for sure when he found out about—

"Frederick."

Nutty looked up. It was Mrs. Ash. She was sitting at the back of the room, her chin resting on her hand, and looking rather out of patience. "What?" Nutty said.

"The minutes are finished. Go ahead."

"Oh, yeah." Nutty got up quickly, and most of the kids started laughing. "Are there any corrections or . . . ah . . . depletions, or whatever you call them."

"Deletions," Mrs. Ash said, and now she couldn't help laughing just a little.

"Right. Does anyone have any?" Nutty looked around. No one said anything. So now was the time. "Okay," he said, "there's something I have to tell you about the Christmas money." His voice was very soft.

"How much did we finally end up with?" Jerry asked, with his usual voice of authority. He was one of the sixth graders who really hated the idea that Nutty, a fifth grader, could have been elected.

"I don't remember the exact amount. It was almost three hundred dollars. But the thing is—"

"Which grade brought in the most?" Jerry again.

"The sixth grade. They had about seventy dollars just by themselves."

"Seventy-four dollars and sixty cents."

"Yeah. Something like that. But—"

"That's exactly how much it was. Didn't you keep records?"

"Not for each class. I just put it all together. It

wasn't a contest or anything."

"That's not the point. There ought to be records."

"We wrote it down," Nutty said, disgusted.

"Jerry," Mrs. Ash said, "please raise your hand when you wish to speak, and then stand up."

"Yes, ma'am. I'm sorry." Jerry raised his hand, and Nutty nodded in his direction. What a jerk. "*Anyone* knows," he said, "that records are *extremely* important when we handle student money. We don't ever want to be accused of mismanagement."

Oh, brother. *Mismanagement.*

"Jerry," Mrs. Ash said, "I think each class kept track of its own total. Nutty—or Frederick—collected it and counted it, and he turned in a total figure. In this case, I believe that is adequate."

Nutty appreciated the support. He knew some other things that Mrs. Ash *could* have said, if she had chosen to.

Jerry was still standing, and his hand was in the air again. "I think, nonetheless, that in the future, Larry, as secretary, should help Nutty with anything of this sort. At least Larry is the type to be careful and make sure everything is done right."

What was this? Nutty looked down to see if Jerry had purple fingers. It was almost as if he knew something. Nutty found himself starting to feel stubborn. How could he admit to anything now? Jerry would use it to get Nutty chased right out of the place.

"That might be a good idea in the future," Mrs. Ash said. "But Frederick's records were all right in this case. There is, however, another matter that he needs to explain to you."

Nutty felt his stomach flop over. He stood there for several seconds, thinking what to do. But he watched Jerry, and he felt his resistance begin to rise again. "Uh . . . Mrs. Ash." She looked up. "I'll take care of that matter myself. I won't need to explain it here."

"Take care of it yourself?" She looked stern, and Nutty was afraid she wasn't going to let him get away with it.

"I'm sure my dad will be willing to help."

There was a long moment in which her better judgment seemed to be fighting her sympathy for Nutty. And then she said, "Well, all right." She probably couldn't stand to think what Jerry would have done.

But Jerry's hand was up. "What is this matter? If it's something that concerns the council, I see no reason why Nutty should handle it himself, even with his father's help."

"That's all right," Mrs. Ash said. "It's not something that needs to be discussed right now."

"But it seems to me—"

"Not now, Jerry. Please sit down. Let's go on to other business."

Nutty watched Jerry. He could see how upset he was, how disappointed. Nutty was almost sure that the guy knew something.

Angela raised her hand. Nutty called on her, and she stood. "Last month we said that if we got enough money, we would give some of our fund to the 'Shoes for Needy Children' campaign. It shouldn't cost too much for the tree and decorations and things we wanted to get, so I move that we give one hundred dollars to that campaign."

"I think we can give a lot more than that," Jerry said, without raising his hand.

Nutty took a breath and tried to relax. At least the subject was changed. "Raise your hand," he said to Jerry.

"But the thing is, Nutty, we don't need that much money for decorations and things."

"You still didn't raise your hand."

"Jerry. Nutty," Mrs. Ash said, "I believe a motion is on the floor."

Nutty looked back at her. "Oh, yeah," he said. "Do we have to vote on that before we can do anything else?"

"First you are supposed to call for a second, and then you can allow discussion."

"Oh, all right. Does anyone want to second the motion?"

"Repeat the motion."

"*Okay*." Boy this kind of stuff could get to be stupid. "The motion was to give one hundred dollars to the fund for needy shoes . . . or, I mean, the fund for needy children, for shoes—or whatever they call it. You know what I mean."

A little second-grade kid named Roger said, "I second the motion." He always did that. He seconded everything. It was the only thing he seemed to understand how to do.

"Okay. Is there any discussion?"

Jerry again. But a fourth-grade girl had her hand up too, so Nutty called on her. The girl stood up and said, "I think it's a good idea."

Brilliant. "Okay." Nutty looked around, but only Jerry was waving his hand around. "Jerry."

"My dad said he would donate a tree. So that saves us some money, and we don't really need a lot of other stuff, especially when there are kids going without shoes. So I think we should give more to the shoes for children fund—a lot more. If you agree with me," he said, gazing around at the kids, "vote *against* Angela's motion. And then I can move that we give *two hundred* dollars—and write a check *today*."

He sat down and then looked straight at Nutty, as if to say, "How would you get out of that one?"

"Look, Jerry," Nutty said, "you're just getting everyone mixed up." But inside, Nutty was all nerves again.

"No I'm not. I'm just—"

"Boys, please. You're forgetting all about Roberts' Rules of Order."

"Okay, okay. So what do I do now?"

"Call for the question."

"The what?"

"Just go ahead and have them vote." Mrs. Ash was starting to sound disgusted.

By now the kids *were* mixed up, but most of them did vote in favor of Angela's motion. Jerry immediately introduced another motion, to add another hundred to the contribution. Roger gave it a second—of course. But Angela argued that it would be better to wait until they knew for sure how much money they had to use for other things before they made that commitment. Then they could just vote to give the whole balance to the fund.

As it turned out Jerry's motion failed, probably because most of the kids liked Angela and didn't like Jerry. Nutty breathed a little easier, but he wanted to get out of there before Jerry tried something else.

"Well, I guess that takes care of things for today," Nutty said.

But Angela raised her hand. "Weren't we going to discuss the menus for the school lunches? And the ski trip?"

"Oh yeah." Nutty really didn't want to get into this right now, but there was not much he could do. "I'm still trying to see what I can do about the cruddy lunches they serve in the cafeteria. Dr. Dunlop told me to write up some menus for him to have a look at. I wrote some down that I thought you might want to look at."

Jerry had his hand up again. "I think," he said, as he stood up, "that our lunches are just fine. And I think Nutty only brought that issue up so he could get elected. Therefore, I see no reason why we should even bother to discuss the matter."

Nutty stared at Jerry for quite some time; and then very calmly he said, "Jerry, I strongly believe that you will not eat so well—or so much—once I *break your face*."

"*Frederick.*"

Nutty got a scolding, but he really didn't care. If he couldn't come up with that money *fast*, he was dead in the water anyway.

But the kids did look at the menus; and before the meeting ended, Angela moved that Nutty's suggestions—with a few changes—be approved. Big deal.

The skiing trip was not so simple. Some of the

kids had suggested a Christmas vacation trip. Nutty had called a travel agent, but he had not followed up after that. He had to admit he hadn't done much.

As soon as the meeting was over, Nutty went to Mrs. Ash. She gave him one day to come up with the money. Nutty told her not to worry, and he told himself to hope Santa came early this year. Then as he walked out, he remembered something else. A very tall sixth grader had promised to kill him right after school. It was not a pleasant thought.

"Oh, I forgot something," he told Mrs. Ash, and he walked back into the room where they had met. As soon as he heard her walk on down the hall, he climbed out the window into the shrubs at the front of the school. When he peeked out, he saw Hobble at the front door, talking to Jerry Robinson. Interesting. He also took a guess that Fowler was in back of the school. Fortunately, there were bushes almost up to the building next to the school. He could make a mad dash to that building and take a very complicated way home.

Chapter IX

Now or Never

Needless to say, it was time to consult with William. But Nutty didn't dare have everyone over to his house. Dad would probably want to attend the meeting and make some menu suggestions of his own. So the meeting was held at Bilbo's house, and Nutty gave his dad the "approved" menus as he walked out the door. Maybe that would satisfy him for a while.

But at Bilbo's, the meeting didn't get off to any better start than the student council meeting had. Everyone was trying to tell William what had happened, and everyone had a different idea about what needed to be done next. Nutty was losing hope. "Maybe I could run away," he told them. "I could join the circus, the way kids do in those old movies."

"It would never work," Orlando said. "With those skinny legs you'd look lousy in tights."

Nutty was about to work Orlando over when William said, "Fellows, that's enough. We must get organized. All this silly talk is getting us nowhere. And actually, we did learn some things today."

"What are you talking about, William?" Nutty said. "The only purple we saw was on *my* thumb."

"Yes, that's right. What does that tell us?"

Nutty thought about that. In fact, he had been thinking about it all day. "I guess it means the guys who broke in used gloves. But gloves wouldn't take *all* the chemical off. Which means I should have gotten some more chemical on my hands when I opened the locker today."

"Very good. So what does that tell us?"

"Someone must have wiped the chemical off," Richie said.

"That's right. And if you think about it, that tells us a good deal. But for right now, let's talk about the symbol. What do you make of the circle?"

The boys sat quietly, all of them concentrating, but no one coming up with anything. Finally Nutty said, "Maybe it just means, 'Hey, we got nothing from you this time—so you get nothing back. Just a big zero.' "

"Perhaps. And yet, I have the feeling that this person is enjoying all this too much to give us nothing at all. We've had a spider and the strange circular shapes. Now a ring around a vanishing symbol and another mark—maybe a dagger. Does anyone see anything, any pattern, in all this?"

"I'll tell you one thing," Nutty said. "I have a hard time believing that Hobble or Fowler would come up with this kind of stuff on their own. Maybe it isn't even them."

"All right," William said. "Let's think about that. Do these symbols connect to someone else? Or is there anyone else who might want to do this?"

"Today, in Student Council, I had the feeling that Jerry Robinson knew something. He was trying to force me to admit that I didn't have all the money. But he doesn't seem the type to sneak around and steal stuff."

"In any case, let's keep him in mind." William leaned back in his chair, mulling things over again. The guys were all sitting on the floor, ringed around him, and they were all waiting and letting him think. Nutty was just hoping something good would come out of William's head soon. Time was running out fast.

Then William looked down at Bilbo. "You haven't said much, Bilbo. What are you thinking?"

"I think this whole thing is pointless now."

"Pointless?"

"Yes. I don't think we can catch the guy. We

might as well forget the whole thing."

Nutty didn't need that, especially since he had the same fears himself.

William thought again, and then he said, "Well, let's not give up quite yet. Who could get into your locker repeatedly, Nutty? What suspects have we overlooked?"

Nutty didn't answer, but Orlando did. "What about Mr. Skinner?" Richie started to laugh. "No, seriously. He's around there every night. He could do it any time. And besides, we saw him open up someone's locker that day we were in the closet."

"Look, Orlando," Nutty said, "an adult isn't going to do something like that."

"What are you talking about? Most crooks are adults."

"Yeah, I know. But they aren't leaving notes and playing little mastermind games—with clues and everything."

"What's this about the locker?" William asked.

"I'm not sure what he was doing," Nutty said. "He was walking down the hall, and he seemed to be looking for a certain locker. I think he was reading the numbers on them, and then he stopped and he had some special key. He opened the locker and looked around in it for a minute or so, and then he just shut it."

"He only opened one?"

"Yeah."

"That's very interesting."

"You don't think he could be the one, do you?"

"Well, that's hard to say. It's worth checking into."

"IIow do we do that?"

"I'm not quite sure. Let me think about it."

"Hey, take your time," Orlando said. "We've got clear until tomorrow before Nutty's head goes on the block."

This, of course, caused Nutty so much discomfort that he was forced to punch Orlando a good shot in the ribs.

"Please, please, fellows. Sometimes you make concentration almost impossible."

"Oh, excuse me," Orlando said, politely. "Next time I'll try to keep my body out of the way of Nutty's fist."

William gave a last, disgusted shake of the head, and then he leaned forward and seemed to go into a trance. Three or four minutes went by before he moved at all. The boys just waited. Nutty figured he better let the genius have his best shot, since time was so short.

"All right," William said, suddenly. "I want to set Skinner up. I think I know how to do that. How many of you can stay with me for a while, let's say, at least for an hour?"

"I can't," Richie said. "My mom told me not to be gone very long."

"What about the rest of you?"

The others said they could stay.

"And how many of you are willing to break into —well, let's say, *sneak* into—the school again?"

There was a moment of silence. Nutty couldn't believe that William would consider such a thing.

"William," Bilbo said, "I don't think that's a good idea."

"Just trust me, Bilbo. I know exactly what I'm doing. I'm sure it's worth the chance."

Bilbo clearly didn't agree, but he only shrugged. And when William got up and reached for his coat, the other guys got up, too. They all got their coats and headed out of the house.

Nutty was walking down the street, trying to think what William was up to. Certain things didn't really make sense to him. He was running everything through his mind again when he looked up and saw two people coming down the sidewalk toward them —the last two people in the world he wanted to see right then.

"Well, hello, Nutty," Hobble said. "You're just the person we're looking for. Your dad told us we might find you over here with Bilbo and all your other little friends."

"What do you want?" Nutty said.

But Fowler was talking. "Well, well, it's little William. What do you need him for these days, Nutty? You must be in some kind of trouble."

Nutty didn't answer, but there was no doubt in Nutty's mind that Fowler knew something. He was gloating.

"And how are you feeling today, Bilbo?" Fowler said. "You guys sure are lucky to be best buddies with the President of the Student Council. Not everyone—"

But Hobble stepped forward, cutting Fowler off. "Nutty, I waited for you after school today. Somehow you got out of the building and got away. Looks like you talk big when you're in the cafeteria, where you know I don't want to punch you out and get myself in trouble again, but you aren't so brave after school."

"Yeah, I'd say that's about right, Hobble. As you see, I'm scared to death of you. I'm quivering in my boots. Now that we've gotten that cleared up, I'm afraid I'll have to be moving on. I have something I have to do. But I *am* glad we had this little talk. I feel much better, don't you?"

Nutty knew he was going to be knocked into

orbit at any moment, but he couldn't help getting in a little sarcasm, a few verbal shots, before the physical ones started coming down on his head.

"Look, you little fifth-grade jerk, you're not getting away with anymore of this kind of stuff." Hobble doubled-up his fists and stepped closer to Nutty. "We're going to fight now."

"Just a moment," William said, and he stepped in front of Nutty.

"Look, William, you stay out of this."

"Oh, believe me, I plan to. But I do have a suggestion to make. We really are busy right now. I was thinking the two of you could go the rounds tomorrow—right after school."

"What's wrong with right now?"

"I told you, we have—"

"Get out of my way." Hobble tried to push William out of the way, but that was a mistake. William grabbed Hobble's arm and sank his fingers into a point just above the elbow. Hobble let out a sharp yelp and then dropped to his knees.

"Don't. Please, don't. Let go."

"Well, now, I could do that of course, but you're so impolite. I offered you a perfectly good—"

"Okay. Tomorrow. I'll fight him tomorrow."

"Excellent." William let go, and Hobble immediately grabbed his elbow and bent forward. He didn't get up for the moment. "I should warn you, however, that I plan to give Nutty a few lessons between now and tomorrow. That's only one of the vulnerable points in the human anatomy that any fighter should know about."

Hobble seemed a whole lot less cocky. He got up, but didn't say anything. It was Fowler who tried to save face. "Jim'll knock all his teeth out," he said.

"Well, we'll see," William said. "But we do have to be going now. It was nice to visit with both of you."

William walked on, and the other boys followed. Nutty thought of some possible insults to drop as he walked away, but he wasn't entirely sure that William could teach him all that much in such a short time. It seemed better just to let well enough alone. After all, he was alive, and that was more than he had expected to be just a few minutes before.

Chapter X

The Break-In

The boys walked straight on to the school. It was after dark now, and Nutty was nervous about trying to sneak in again. But William went to the front doors, tried each and found them locked, then started pounding on one. "Help me out, fellows," he said. "Bang on the doors as hard as you can."

"He'll kill you," Orlando said.

"Well, let's say he'll be very angry. But that's fine."

And so the boys pounded away on the doors, rattling them until the building seemed to shake. And finally Mr. Skinner showed up. "What's going on," he said, his voice fierce.

"Excuse me, sir," William said. "We need to get to a locker."

Skinner was looking at Nutty, not at William. "Now look." He pointed a gritty finger at Nutty. "I told you before—stay away from this school at night. I don't know what you—"

"But this is *very* important, sir," William said. "It has to do with some money that may have been stolen. If we could just—"

"Money? What money?"

"There was some money—quite a sum of it—in Nutty's locker. He needs to check on it."

"No way. Now you kids just clear out."

"But some of it is missing. We need to make a thorough search of his locker and make sure it isn't there."

So much for William's vow of honesty.

"He can look in the morning."

"But it's almost a hundred dollars. If people are getting into the lockers here at the school, I think you have yourself quite a problem."

"*I* do?"

"Yes, sir."

"Look, it's not my problem. If Nutsell can't hang on to his—"

"Well, all right. We'll just go down to the police station then. We might as well report it."

"Are you sure you didn't just lose it?" He was looking at Nutty again.

"No, I didn't lose it," Nutty said.

William spoke quickly. "There's still a slight chance it just slipped down in his locker, I guess.

That's why we need to check."

Skinner stared at William for some time; then he looked over at Nutty again. "Well, okay. Come on. You others stay here."

But William said, "Could I come along, sir?"

"What for?"

"Well, frankly, I need—*very* badly—to stop at the boys' restroom."

Skinner shook his head. "For crying out loud," he said, and Nutty thought maybe he almost smiled. "All right. Come on."

And so the two boys walked down the dimly lighted hallway with Mr. Skinner. Nutty had no idea what William was trying to do, but he carried out his part. He pretended to make a search of his locker, while Mr. Skinner stood and watched, and William was in the restroom.

"Nothing there?" Skinner asked, and he actually seemed rather concerned.

"No. I can't see it."

"Oh, boy, that's all we need around here. Dr. Dunlop is going to hit the ceiling."

"Yeah, I guess so," Nutty said, and he couldn't think for the life of him why William had wanted Skinner to know. By morning everything would be out in the open.

William came out of the boys' room at that point and walked over to Nutty. "Nothing?" he said.

"Nope." Nutty shook his head and looked as convincing as he could.

"What were you doing with that kind of money in there anyway?" Skinner said.

"It was the Christmas Fund money," William said, before Nutty could answer. "It takes an *evil* person to steal something like that."

"And it takes a *dumb* one to leave it in his locker," Skinner said. Then he turned and started walking back up the hall. "Come on, boys. You get out of here now."

Nutty and William followed him; but when they got to the doors, William didn't go all the way out. He stopped and said, "One thing you might watch for, Mr. Skinner: the guy who did it left some kind of mark on the locker. He must think he's some sort of mastermind. He might try to come back and leave another clue. So you ought to keep an eye out for him."

"There ain't nobody coming in here. I've got *all* the doors locked. So don't worry about that."

"Well, this guy seems to think he's smarter than other people. There's no telling what he might try."

"Look, I don't care about any of that. I just clean up in here. You talk to Dr. Dunlop about all that."

And so William shut the door, and the boys walked away; but when they got to the sidewalk

William said, "Okay, fellows, follow me." He made a wide circle across the front lawn and then into the bushes by the front of the building.

"What's going on?" Nutty said.

"All right. Let me explain—briefly." The boys crouched next to the building, close to each other, and William whispered.

"If he's our man, he might try one of two things. He might be getting nervous, and he might put the money back—and make it look as if it slipped down to the bottom perhaps. Or what I said might have challenged him. He might want to drop us another clue."

"Would he be that stupid?" Bilbo said.

"I think so. Our thief—whoever it is—obviously believes himself to be very clever. But he's not as smart as he thinks."

"Skinner acted pretty nervous, didn't he?" Orlando said.

"Yes, he did. We just might be on to something." William paused for a moment, and then he said, "All right, now listen. I opened the window to the boys' room. We'll all climb in. And we're going to watch Nutty's locker. Two of us will go down to the closet again. Nutty and I can do that. I'm small and Nutty's thin. We could fit in the trash barrel if we had to."

90

"Have fun," Orlando said.

William ignored him. "Bilbo, you and Orlando stay in the restroom. If you see him coming, you can climb back out the window very quickly."

"Why don't we all just stay in the bathroom?" Nutty said.

"I already considered that. It could take some time for all of us to get out the window. Besides that, we need two witnesses, from two vantage points, so that our case will be unquestionable. But we can only look out the doors one at a time."

"This is really dangerous," Bilbo said.

William gave no rebuttal. "All right," he said. "We need to catch the thief tonight if we can. So let's all use our heads. If we get split up, meet back at Bilbo's house."

And so the boys climbed in the window, as silently as possible, and then William—with extreme care—opened the door a crack. He finally peeked all the way out and then motioned for Nutty to follow him. The two boys tiptoed down the hall as quickly as they could. Nutty was terrified. His feet sounded like scraping sandpaper in his own ears. At any moment he expected to see Skinner standing in the shadows, or to hear his voice come booming through the hall.

But the boys made it to the closet, and they got

inside quickly. Nutty took a long breath, and then he just stood there, hoping his eyes would grow accustomed to the dark. No such luck. It was absolutely black in the little room.

William waited for maybe half a minute, let his breath become even, and then he cracked the door open, ever so slightly. "Do you understand what's happening?" he whispered to Nutty.

"What do you mean?"

"Don't you see what I'm trying to do?"

"I guess so. You said outside that you—"

"No, Nutty. Come on—*think*."

This was really confusing to Nutty. He let the whole matter run through his mind again. What had William said outside? Did it make sense? There were things that *did* trouble Nutty. Finally he said, "William, I still have a hard time believing that Skinner is the thief."

"Why?"

"Some of the things he said sounded too real— like he really was surprised. And besides that, I can't picture him doing any of this stuff."

"Maybe the clues are a cover to make it look like something he wouldn't do."

"Could be, I guess. But I don't think so."

William let the silence settle in for a time, let Nutty think a while longer, and then he said, "But

Nutty, I think your analysis is probably right."

"You mean you don't think Skinner did it either?"

"I didn't say that. But if he didn't, who did?"

"I don't know, William. Hobble and Fowler do seem to know something. Fowler sounded like he was—"

"Sssshhhh. Don't talk so loudly. Does no one else occur to you?"

"No." He thought for a time again. "And I really don't see what we're doing in here."

"We're here to catch the thief—if we can."

Nutty was baffled. He tried hard to think what William was up to. "The only thing I can see for sure is that we're in here for some reason other than the one you gave us outside."

"That's right."

"I thought you said you didn't believe in lying."

"I don't, Nutty. But I can't catch a thief without using some deception. I'm fighting fire with fire."

"But can't you tell *me* what's going on?"

"I'd like to, Nutty. But I don't think you're ready yet. You just wouldn't believe me if I told you what I'm thinking. I hate to believe it myself."

Chapter XI

Kept in the Dark

William and Nutty took turns watching through the crack, but no one appeared in the hallway. Apparently Mr. Skinner was working in another part of the building. Nutty was a little angry with William for not being willing to say more, but, on the other hand, he wasn't sure he really wanted to know what the little genius was suspecting.

Nutty was leaning against the trash barrel when a thought struck him. It had begun with the notice of a slight odor in the room. He opened the lid to the barrel and reached in. "Oh no," he said.

"What's the matter?"

"This barrel is almost full of trash."

"I know. I checked it right after we got in here."

"Why didn't you say anything?"

"I didn't want to worry you."

"What will we do if he comes down here?"

"Well—sooner or later—he's bound to. Most of his equipment is here. So, if he does, just do what I tell you to do, all right?"

"Come on, William. Quit being so bossy. Just tell me what you have in mind. Maybe I'll have a better idea."

William didn't answer, and Nutty sensed that something had just happened. William had seemed to start. Nutty had felt the movement even in the dark.

"What's the matter?"

"It's Skinner. He's at the other end of the hall, and I think—yes—he's coming this way."

"Oh, criminy, William, we're trapped. What'll we do?"

"We're trapped all right," William said, but his tone was strange, as though he rather liked the idea.

"Come on, William. Let's run now. We can head for the back doors."

"No, wait."

"What do you mean, wait?" Nutty pushed closer to the door, wanted to push William right on out. Standing there in the dark, just waiting to be caught, was almost more than he could stand. "Come on, William. Let's run—now."

"He stopped. He's opening your locker. Take a look."

William moved back, and Nutty looked out the crack. Sure enough, Skinner was in front of Nutty's locker, peering inside. And then he began to rummage around, seeming to search for something. "He *is* the thief."

"It does look that way, doesn't it?"

"Maybe he's going to leave a clue." Nutty watched closely, but Skinner only seemed to look around inside, and then he shut the door. "Oh, no," Nutty gasped, "he's coming this way again."

William grabbed Nutty's shoulder and pulled him back. "Let me see."

"No, come on. Let's get out of here."

"Wait until I give the signal. I'll throw open the door and when I do, run right past him. He won't expect it, and he's not fast. Just head for the front doors as fast as you can run."

"What about you?"

"Get ready." There was a horrible pause. Nutty could feel his pulse pounding through his whole body. Any second now Skinner would be there . . . and then William threw open the door and said, "Run, Nutty, run."

Nutty bolted out the door and right into Skinner. He slammed into the man's chest, hitting him hard. Skinner stumbled back and Nutty went spinning to one side. But he managed to catch his balance before he fell down, and he was off and running before Skinner could recover.

Skinner let out with a curse, and then he yelled, "Hey, you—come back here." But Nutty was flying now. He got to the front doors way ahead of Skinner, and he went tumbling outside. For a moment he wasn't sure which way to run, but then he thought better of running out across the front lawn where he could be seen. He turned sharply to his left and ran along the front of the building, close to the shrubs. He just wanted to make it to the corner of the building and on past before Skinner came out the front doors.

And then something strange happened. He heard a voice—not someone yelling, not someone chasing him. A voice speaking softly, and close to him. Maybe in the bushes. For a moment, in his confusion, he thought it was Orlando or Bilbo. He spun around, never really stopping, but running sideways and looking back. A head poked out from the shrubs, and then another. "Come on, you guys," Nutty gasped, "he caught us in the closet."

The heads popped back into the bushes. By now Nutty had almost stopped. And then he knew it was someone else, not his friends. Orlando and Bilbo had to be on the other side of the front doors. And they wouldn't jump back when he spoke to them. Suddenly Nutty was running full speed again. This was just one more complication, one more fear.

He ran hard, all the way to Bilbo's, long after he could have slowed. It just felt better to keep pushing, moving, not waiting in the dark. But when he got to Bilbo's, he realized that he had to be way ahead of the other guys—*if* they had all gotten out of the building. And by now he was starting to think of a lot of things that he hadn't bothered with when he was just trying to get away.

It was cold out, but Nutty was still warm from running. He sat down on the front steps and tried to catch his breath. He was in trouble. He knew that now. In fact, running had been almost pointless. It was just something he hadn't been able to resist. But why was he so sure that Skinner had recognized him?

He thought about that, and then he remembered: William had spoken right out loud. "Run, Nutty, run," he had said, and not in a whisper. Skinner had to have heard it.

Why? Why would William do something that stupid? It wasn't like him at all. And where had William gone? Why hadn't he run, too? Skinner had heard him, knew there was another kid in the closet. Once he had seen Nutty get away, he would go back looking for William. What sense did that make? A thought crossed Nutty's mind, but it was too stupid—too impossible—to believe.

It was another few minutes before Bilbo and Orlando showed up. They had slowed to a walk before they had gotten there, and they weren't out of breath. "Nutty," Orlando said, when he saw him on the steps, "where's William?"

"I don't know."

"What do you mean? Didn't he run with you?"

"No. He told me to make a break for it. I took off and ran right into Skinner. But then I got past him, and he started to chase me and—"

"We knew all that. We saw what happened. Or at least we heard it. But we thought William ran with you."

"We shut the door when we heard all the racket," Orlando said. "And I headed out the window. We just thought both of you made a run for it."

"Wasn't that you two in the bushes? The ones I talked to?"

"Huh?"

"Never mind. That's what I thought." Nutty was thinking fast. There were all kinds of loose ends he couldn't figure out. "How did you guys know I made it out?"

"I went back and checked," Bilbo said. "When Orlando was climbing out, I realized Skinner had gone by our door—I heard his big shoes go tromping by—and so I looked out to make sure he hadn't caught you. I waited until I could see that Skinner was coming back without you. He was way down the hall, and it was pretty dark; but when I could see that he was alone, and he wasn't saying anything, I went ahead and left."

"But you didn't see William?"

"No. I don't know what happened to him."

"Maybe he waited until Skinner chased you," Orlando said, "and then he headed for the back doors."

"Yeah. That would make sense." And yet, something in the idea disturbed Nutty. Maybe William had sacrificed Nutty to save himself. But he said nothing to Bilbo and Orlando. He didn't want them jumping to any conclusion—conclusions Nutty himself didn't like to consider.

And so he kept quiet, and the three boys stayed where they were, waiting out front, worrying. After a time Orlando walked out to the front of the yard and looked down the street. "Hey, it's William," he said. "He's just down the block a little ways."

Orlando started walking in that direction, and Nutty and Bilbo hurried after. They met William several houses down the street. "What happened?" Nutty said. "Did he catch you?"

"Well, yes. I'm afraid he did. But I did some fast talking. We should be all right."

"Fast talking? What did you say?"

"Essentially, I told the truth: that we were trying to catch the thief."

"What will they do to us?" Orlando said, and he sounded scared.

"I didn't mention anything about you two. There seemed no reason to do so. Nutty, of course, will have to go in to see Dunlop in the morning." He turned and looked at Nutty. "I'll go with you," he said. "I think I can handle that situation all right."

"Then he knows it was Nutty who got away?"

"Yes, I'm afraid so."

"Did he recognize him?"

"I'm not sure. But it didn't matter. I spoke Nutty's name when I opened the door. It was a stupid mistake on my part."

Orlando would normally have made some comment to a line like that, but he must have been too nervous. And no one else said anything. It was suddenly very quiet outside.

"Oh, man," Nutty finally said, "Dunlop's going to carve me up and have me for dinner now."

"Maybe not," William said. "Maybe not. Not if we catch the culprit."

"Hey, that's right," Nutty said. "We saw Skinner open my locker. Did you guys see it, too?"

"*I* did," Bilbo said. "It was kind of dark, but I could see him."

"Then we've got him." Nutty looked down at William, who was looking back up, his arms folded across his chest. "We have him, don't we?"

"That depends on how you look at it, Nutty. I know what I saw tonight, but I don't know whether anyone else will believe me. I have a hard time believing it myself."

"What do you mean, what *you* saw? We all saw the same thing."

"No, Nutty, things are never *that* simple. Just because we all look at the same thing doesn't mean we *see* the same thing."

Nutty thought about that. He tried to think what William was getting at. And then something else occurred to him. "William, there were other people around that building tonight. Now that I think about it, it might have been Hobble and Fowler. They were out in the bushes in front of the building. And they saw me."

"Yes, that doesn't surprise me. They followed us to the school, you know."

"No, I didn't know. Why didn't you say something?"

"There was no reason to complicate matters. We had enough to worry about. But it makes my point, doesn't it?"

"What point?"

"We all look, but some see more than others."
He looked at Orlando and then at Bilbo. "And sometimes we assume that others see as poorly as we do."

But Nutty had no time for such philosophizing.
That was fine for William. But Nutty had to face the
music in the morning.

Chapter XII

Dunlop's Office

Nutty had trouble sleeping. By morning he was just glad to be getting the whole thing over with. He was a cooked goose, but at least it was time to get out of the oven. At breakfast, however, things got a little more complicated. The phone rang, and Dad answered. Nutty didn't pay much attention until he heard Mr. Nutsell say, "Yes, Dr. Dunlop, I can make a little time to come over. I think my wife can too."

This had to come sooner or later too, Nutty supposed, and he might as well get the whole mess cleared up at one time. But when Dad got off the phone, he wanted to know what was going on. "Going on?" Nutty said, stalling.

"Yes. You know what I'm talking about. Why does Dr. Dunlop want to see us?"

"Well, it has to do with . . . look, I'd rather not

explain it all twice. Why don't we just wait until we get down there."

Dad got that sick, oh-don't-let-this-happen-to-me look on his face; Susie started saying, "I'll bet he's in trouble again"; and Mom just muttered, "I really don't need this today." But Nutty managed not to say exactly what was going on, in spite of plenty of questions from Dad.

The Nutsells were silent as they drove to the school, however. It was like the drive to the cemetary, after a funeral. Dad had decided to wait, but he was obviously expecting the worst.

At the office, the secretary told the Nutsells to go right in. But the big surprise was that William was already there. He was sitting with his arms folded, leaning back, his legs dangling from the rather high chair. And across from him was Dunlop, at his desk, trying to pretend that William didn't exist.

As soon as Dunlop looked up, he assumed the manner and voice he always used on parents. He spoke almost sweetly, saying, "Please, sit down." And once they had done so, "I'm afraid a little problem has come up. It seems the boys entered the school last night. I suppose your son told you about that?"

"No." They both spoke at the same time, and then they both looked at Nutty.

"Yes, well, it's the sort of thing we cannot tolerate, especially since it involved illegal entry through a window. We could, if we chose to, view it as a criminal act."

"Freddie," Mrs. Nutsell said, "I can't believe you would do such a thing."

"It's not what you think, Mom. We were trying to catch a thief."

"A thief?"

"Yes, yes," Dunlop said, and he lowered his head to look over his bifocals, "that is why I called you in this morning. The custodian said the boys had quite a story to tell. Frankly, he thought it was all an invention on the part of Bilks here, which may, of course, be correct. William caused a good deal of trouble during the brief period he attended this school, and I have a feeling he's at the bottom of all this."

He spoke as though William weren't even there, but William spoke up. "That's right. I am," he said, and he smiled.

Dunlop looked at him about the way Nutty looked at the food served in the school cafeteria every day.

At that point, however, Nutty felt he had to clear some things up. And so he told his story, the whole thing, complete with the symbols on the locker and all the plans to trap the crook.

"Now wait a minute," Dunlop said at the end, "you keep claiming that you know who the thief is. If so, name him, and I'll see what can be done."

That was one thing Nutty had held back. He was not really sure what William wanted to do about that. He glanced at William and got a little shake of the head. "We can't say that yet. We can't prove it to you yet. But we know who it is."

"Freddie, now don't do that," Mr. Nutsell said. "That's how you got yourself in trouble in the first place, trying to handle this whole thing on your own."

"I know. But no one would have done anything. We've, or at least William, has solved the crime. We just need a little more evidence. Right now no one would believe us. It's someone that no one would think of."

Dr. Dunlop cleared his throat. Something important was coming. "Bilks."

"Yes."

"You have been a problem to me before. Now you have returned, broken into our school, and you have obviously been a terrible influence on Frederick Nutsell and some of the other boys. Frederick and I were just getting so we could work together, and he was showing signs of being an excellent Student Council President. Now this has happened. I consider—"

"I'm sorry you look at it that way, sir. I came here to help get your Christmas Fund money back."

"That may *sound* good, but you have failed. And you have caused a good deal of trouble in the process. I hope you have learned that you can't take such matters into your own hands. Now if you want to save yourself from criminal prosecution, you will tell me who it is you think stole the money."

William didn't answer for a time, just looked back at Dr. Dunlop; and then he said, "I really can't do that right now."

"Can't do what?"

"Can't tell you who the thief is."

"And why not?"

"Actually, I can't give you my reasons either."

"Then I'll just go ahead and call the police. I hadn't wanted to deal with the two of you that way. But after all, you did break and enter the building last night."

William didn't move, didn't blink, just looked back at Dunlop. Nutty couldn't take it. "No, don't call the police," he said. "It's Mr. Skinner."

"*What* is Mr. Skinner, Frederick?"

"He's the thief."

Slowly a smile spread across Dr. Dunlop's face, that oh-I'm-so-much-smarter-than-you look of his. "The custodian? The man we've had around here for over ten years? He's suddenly decided to take up a life of crime and steal the Christmas Fund from needy children?"

It did sound a little unlikely when Dunlop put it that way. "I guess so," Nutty said. "We saw him open my locker last night."

This did not seem to surprise Dunlop at all. In fact, the smile returned, magnified. "Frederick, the man told me that. He explained that he thought it good to search it one more time, just to make sure the money hadn't slipped down behind something."

"Well, we saw him look in another locker besides, another time."

"You were in the school *another* time?"

That was something else Nutty had left out of the first story. "We didn't break in that time. It was just after school. But we saw him open a locker and look in."

"That is part of his job, Frederick. I have told him to spot-check the lockers from time to time."

"Is that legal?" William asked.

"Certainly." But Dunlop suddenly sounded less sure of himself. "He wouldn't do it otherwise."

Now William produced his own "wise" smile, but he said nothing.

"Now listen, young man," Dunlop said, "I'm very unhappy about this whole matter. You come in here and lead our boys on a wild goose chase, and then you accuse a trusted employee, a man who never stole a dime in his life."

So the goose had finally arrived—a wild one. And Nutty knew it was roasting time. But the last thing he expected was William's next statement.

"Dr. Dunlop, Mr. Skinner is not the thief. I know that."

"But you said—"

"No, sir. That was Nutty's opinion. I don't share it."

Nutty stared at William, and both the Nutsells stared at Nutty. Meanwhile, Dunlop was still zeroed in on William. "Well, now, it seems you two better get your stories together. Maybe it *is* time to call the police."

"No, wait a minute," Mr. Nutsell said. "Let me suggest something else. I would like this whole thing not to go out of this office. *I* will assume financial responsibility. I'll pay back the eighty dollars. And Freddie will earn every penny of it back by working for me."

"Well, that *is* very generous, Mr. Nutsell. Maybe we can solve the problem that easily. Frederick is basically a good boy. He just lets himself be influenced by a certain young man with an overactive imagination." He directed a grim look at William again.

William smiled politely, and he nodded to Dr. Dunlop.

Nutty was the one who was upset. Dad was just buying him off; no one really believed his story. And what was with William? Was nothing what it really seemed? How could a guy tell what the truth was— even when he had taken a good look at it?

Now Dunlop was saying, "Well, then, that settles it," and Dad was promising a check by Monday. Then they were all getting up to leave. But nothing was settled—not really. There was still some crook out there thinking he was a mastermind, and maybe just waiting to attack Nutty again.

And then something occurred to Nutty. But the connection to what had just been going on was not all clear in his own mind. "Just a second," he said. "Dr. Dunlop, I have those menus in my notebook. Will you look at them?"

"Well, yes . . . I suppose—"

"Freddie," Mrs. Nutsell said, "I don't think now is the time to get into that."

"Will you look at them, Dr. Dunlop?"

"Yes, of course. I told you before that I would." Dunlop smiled at Nutty, and then at the parents. "I'm always happy to hear suggestions from the children, especially the President of the Student Council."

"Will you use these then?"

"Well we'll have to see. One never knows for sure."

Nutty was about to push the matter harder when he felt a firm hand on his shoulder. Suddenly he was on his way out the door, under his father's tender guidance.

"For heaven's sake," Dad said, or rather whispered, as they got to the outer office. "You have a lot to learn about timing."

"Dad, I'm tired of *timing*"

"What?"

"I'm tired of tricks and everything making no sense. I want something to be straight out, and right."

"Freddie, I don't know what you're talking about. I just saved you. You're lucky still to be Student Council President. Just remember that." He turned and walked out into the hallway, and then he waited for Nutty to follow.

But there was William patting Nutty on the shoulder. "Don't worry," he said, "everything is working out fine."

"William, what are you talking about? What are you trying to do to me? I thought you were my friend."

"Oh, believe me, I am."

"Don't tell me to *believe* you. I don't know what to believe."

Chapter XIII

Things Are Not What They Seem

Mom and Dad left after imparting a few last gems of wisdom—not to mention a few threats—but William stayed behind. "Nutty," he said, "get the fellows to meet out in back of the building just as soon as you're out of school this afternoon. I'll be here, and we'll see if we can't get this whole thing straightened out."

"William, are you nuts? First, you say—"

"Nutty, we don't have time to talk now. Everything I've done makes sense. You'll understand before the day is over. Honest."

"Honest? How can you even say the word? You lied to me."

"When?"

"Last night. You said Skinner was the thief."

"No. I never said that. I said it would appear so. You were the one who said it *was* so."

Nutty just stood there. The whole thing was getting crazier every second.

"Listen, Nutty, we still have a chance of catching the thief. I know some things that you don't. But we can't talk now. I'll see you this afternoon at three-fifteen." And away he went.

A little later Nutty remembered that Hobble was planning to dismember him that afternoon. This was no small problem, especially since William had never gotten around to those fighting lessons. Nutty figured his best shot was to get to William just as soon as the bell rang. Maybe they could at least get another stay of execution.

And so when school was out that day Nutty headed, with his friends, directly to the playground out back. William was already there, sitting in a swing. If Dunlop caught him out there, he would have him "doing time."

But right now Nutty was a lot more concerned about clearing up all the confusion, maybe even solving the crime. "All right, what do we do now?" he said to William.

"First, we need to think some things through together."

"William, you said you knew some things that I didn't. Tell me what that is first."

"We'll get to that, Nutty. For a minute I want to get back to the clues. I want to—"

"Oh, come on," Orlando said. "We've been all through that stuff."

"Be patient, Orlando. Be patient." William pushed back with his toes on the ground, and then he swung forward a little. "Let's call the last mark a dagger, or maybe a sword. That's what it seems to be. We have a spider; a pattern of circles that might be back-to-back letter B's; a ring around a vanishing symbol; and then a sword. Does anyone else see a pattern in that besides me?"

William looked at each boy, and they all seemed to be thinking, but no lights seemed to be coming on. Finally Nutty said, "The spider and bees both have stingers. We mentioned that before. Maybe the sword is like a stinger too. But I don't know about the circle. And I don't see what that all tells us anyway."

"But you are seeing something I'm seeing, and I have the feeling we're on the edge of a discovery. Do any of you see anything more in it?"

"Come on, William," Richie said. "Just tell us what *you* think."

"Not yet. I would like, if possible, for one of

you to see it. That way I can be certain I'm not dreaming dreams. Of course, I do have the advantage of having seen the criminal last night—or at least I think I did."

"You *saw* him?"

"Perhaps."

"We're not back to Mr. Skinner again, are we?" Richie asked.

"No, no. Not Skinner."

"William, enough is enough," Nutty said. "If you saw him, just tell us who it is."

"Well, I still want to be careful. Sometimes we think we know what we have seen and yet it's a distortion of some sort. We found that out last night. I thought maybe one of you could tell me something that would alter my view, convince me I didn't see exactly what I thought I saw."

"William, for crying out loud," Nutty said, "I don't think you even know what you're talking about. You're just bluffing. I was in the closet with you. The only person we saw was Mr. Skinner."

"Yes, at *that* time." William sat for a moment, looking down at the ground. Then he said, "All right. I suppose I will have to be a little more forthright with you. You see, I set things up last night. I knew Skinner would come down to his closet sooner or later, and that's why I went there. I had Nutty make his dash primarily to make a ruckus and to give the impression that both of us had cleared out. I yelled Nutty's name so that Skinner would be all the more angered and likely to chase after him. I, of course, stayed in the closet and waited—and watched. It meant giving myself up to Skinner, but I gambled that it would be worth it, that I would see the thief."

"Wait a minute," Orlando said. "What made you so sure that the thief would just happen to be in the building?"

"Let's just say that I had no doubt about that. I had made arrangements ahead of time."

"Hey . . ." Nutty said, and he thought for a moment. "Are we talking about Hobble and Fowler? I think I saw them out in front last night."

"If they were out in front during the very time I saw what I saw . . ." He didn't finish his sentence.

"Then you're saying they are *not* the criminals?"

"Well, I would have to say they *appear* not to be."

"Oh, brother," Nutty said. He shook his head, and then he plopped down on the grass, as if to say, "I give up."

William let some time pass, and he kept looking from one boy to another. Finally Bilbo said, "William, there's something you haven't considered. Maybe all the clues, and everything you say you have seen, were designed to throw you off. Sometimes logical thinking still leads to the wrong conclusion."

"Yes, yes. Very good. That's exactly what I've been telling myself—even hoping—ever since I first began to understand the clues."

"But now you have no doubt about who it is?"

William let the swing rock forward and back again. He considered. "Let's say, I am willing to be proved wrong. I would welcome information that would change my thinking." William waited some time again, but no one responded. "Well, okay," he said, suddenly. "I guess that gives us all something to think about. Let's go home."

"Home?" Nutty said. "Come on, William. You haven't really told us anything. You said you thought you could clear everything up today."

"I guess I was overly optimistic."

"Oh, man." Nutty flopped over on his back. "William, you're going to drive me out of my mind."

"Well, I'm sorry. I'm doing my best. You fellows do expect too much of me sometimes, you know."

Nutty moaned, and then he got up very slowly. "William, I just want a straight answer. I'm tired of all these games we've been playing."

"Well, I'll tell you what. I'll walk home with you, and on the way I'll try to clarify any apparent inconsistencies in my behavior."

So the boys went their separate ways, William and Nutty walked around to the front of the school. And there they found that they had walked directly into the paths of one Mr. Hobble and one Mr. Fowler. Somehow Nutty—and William—had managed to forget about those two.

"All right, Nutty," Hobble said. "This is it."

"Oh, wait," William said. "I did promise that we, or Nutty would go the rounds with you today. But I'm afraid we are going to have to delay that just a bit. If you would go to your house, Jim, and wait there, we'll contact you in about an hour. How would that be?"

"Look, I—"

But William raised his little claw and reached toward Hobble.

"No, wait. I'm not fighting you. I'm fighting Nutty."

"Oh, I know. But you wouldn't mind waiting just another hour would you?"

"Yeah, he would," Fowler said. "He don't have to—"

But Hobble said, "All right. All right. But just call me at my house; don't come over. We'll meet somewhere else."

"Excellent," William said. "That's just what I had in mind."

Away went William, and Nutty hurried along

behind. "William, what are you doing? What good is an hour going to do?"

"Oh, Nutty, in the next hour lots of things could happen."

"Like what?"

But William continued to walk until the two of them had turned the corner. Then he said, "All right, stop."

"What?"

"Stop a minute. Nutty, have you ever read *The Hobbit*?"

"No."

"Well, if you had, you would know the scene where Bilbo Baggins faces his first great adventure. He runs from a gang of spiders, but then he doubles back. He sneaks back around behind them and returns to help his friends, the dwarves. Wait just a minute or two, and then we'll double back. Maybe we'll trick a spider or two."

Chapter XIV

The Spider and the Web

"William, you're taking a big chance," Nutty said as they approached the school. "If Dunlop sees you, or if Skinner does, you'll be in big trouble."

"You'll walk ahead and let me know when the coast is clear. I'm not worried."

"Walk ahead where? Where are we going?"

"Well—would you rather hide in the closet again, or in the restroom?"

"Holy cow, William. You're not starting that kind of stuff again, are you?"

"Just this one last time."

"But what if we get caught again?"

"You have a point. The restroom might be better. They can't say a whole lot about our being in there."

"They can about *you* being there."

"Never mind about that. Just go in and take a look down the hall."

Nutty did just that, and when he came out, he said, "Okay, hurry. I don't see Dunlop or Skinner."

"Anyone else?"

"Just a couple of fourth-grade kids."

"That's okay. Let's go." And so the two of them hurried on past the main office and down the hall to the boys' room. When they got inside, William cracked the door and set up his watch. "It could be a little while yet," he said.

Nutty just shook his head. He was tired of trying to figure all this out. But he took turns watching with William, and once they had to hurry and hide in the stalls when Skinner came walking by. It was a few minutes after that when William said, "Okay. Come here. Hurry."

Nutty hurried to the door. William had let it go shut. "All right. Count to ten, and then open it—very slowly."

Nutty did exactly as he was told, and then he said, "What the heck?"

"Do you see someone?"

"Sure."

"What's he doing?"

"He's opening my locker."

"All right. Don't move yet. Wait and see what he does."

"He's putting something inside."

"All right. Let's go. Walk out and say hello to him."

"William, what's going on? He's not the thief."

"Just do it."

So out they went, and the two of them walked straight down the hall toward Nutty's locker. "Hey, Bilbo," Nutty said. "What are you doing?"

Bilbo had just shut the locker, and now he spun around. "Nutty!" His face turned white.

"What are you doing?"

"Nothing. I just . . . ah . . ."

"How did you get my locker open?"

"I know your combination. You told me what it was."

"I did?"

And now the two were just staring at each other, and all the truth was pouring in on Nutty. But it was impossible. There had to be some other explanation.

"What did you just put in there?" Nutty said.

Bilbo didn't speak for some time; then finally he shrugged and said, "Nutty, it's the money."

"*You* took it?"

"It was just a joke. The whole thing was just

to play a trick on you. I was always going to bring it back." Bilbo tried to laugh.

"What do you mean, Bilbo? You know what I've been going through the last few days."

"I know," Bilbo said, and he looked down at the floor. "This whole thing got all messed up. It did start out as a joke. But I'm not the thief—not really. I just put eighty dollars in your locker, but it's out of my own savings. I'm not the one who ended up with your money."

"Who is?" William said. "That's what I was trying to get you to say this afternoon."

"I know. I could tell that you were on to me."

"Wait a minute," Nutty said. "You guys seem to know a bunch of stuff that I don't. I thought you said you weren't the thief."

"Look," Bilbo said, and he was looking down at the floor again. "I'll explain what I can. I'm not sure that you're going to believe me though."

"I think the first thing we better do is get out of this hallway," William said. "It's not safe for me to be here."

"You're right," Nutty said, and the three boys walked down the hall and out the back door. Then they went to the far corner of the playground and sat down on the grass. "Okay," Nutty said. "You better explain everything, because I'm pretty confused right now."

Bilbo nodded, but he seemed to think things over before he spoke. "All right. I was sitting at my desk that morning when you came flying in late and threw the money bag in your locker. I couldn't believe you would do that, Nutty. If you're going to be a decent president, you've got to be more responsible. I decided I'd teach you a lesson."

"So did you take the money right then?" William asked.

"Yes. I waited for a while, and then I asked Mrs. Smiley if I could go to the restroom. There was nothing to it from that point. I knew Nutty's combination. He had given it to me himself one time. And no one could see me. Or even if they did, they would just think I was at my own locker."

"Why did you only take the twenties?" Nutty asked.

"It just hit me as a good idea. I didn't want to take every penny and scare you to death. I just wanted to make you sweat a little before I gave it all back."

"But why did you wait so long?"

"Yeah, well . . . everything got messed up. But I can't say anything about that."

"Come on, Bilbo. Who ended up with the money?"

Bilbo took a breath, and then he glanced toward the school, almost as if he were afraid. "A lot of this was *your* fault," Bilbo said, and he looked at William.

"My fault?"

"Yeah. I didn't put any spider in those shoes. But you were so hot to make something out of it. And you started all that stuff about outwitting the thief. I just thought I'd lead you around for a day or two and show you that someone else has some brains around here."

"I did, however, break your code."

"Sure, but it wasn't that tough. Those last two clues were obvious on purpose."

"Wait a minute," Nutty said. "What do you mean they were obvious?"

"Let William tell you."

Nutty looked over at William.

"Well," William said, "I started with different assumptions, and so I saw different implications in the clues. You assumed an enemy was out to get you, but I immediately considered your friends. I saw from the beginning that the thief seemed to be some- one who had your trust, someone who knew your comings and goings. And then when the thief wiped the chemical from the handle, I knew it had to be one of our inner circle."

"But what did the clues mean?"

"I wasn't sure about the spider, and now I find there was nothing in it at first, though it tied in later.

The B's were a bit too easy, however. Bilbo himself suggested that the circles were back-to-back B's. That was a bit of overconfidence on his part. I thought of your friends, and I immediately saw Bilbo Baggins the Burglar in those letters. The spider fit with that— as I told you this afternoon."

"What were the other two marks?"

"Bilbo Baggins possessed a ring that made him disappear when he put it on. The B's disappeared when the ring was put around them. And the sword represented Bilbo Baggins's weapon, 'the sting.'"

Nutty nodded. He could see it now. "But when did you do all this stuff?" he asked Bilbo.

"Well, when you and Orlando got in the closet that first time, I told Richie to walk on ahead of me. As soon as he walked down the hallway, I hurried over and put the B's on the locker, and then I came back and told you guys I was leaving."

"What did you write with?"

"Just some chalk I had with me. I had it in my pocket because I was waiting for a chance to give you a clue."

"That all brings us back to the *real* question, Bilbo." Bilbo looked over at William. "Why did you wait so long to return the money?"

"I didn't. I went back to the locker after school that next day. I put the symbols on the inside and outside—just to give you plenty to go on. And then I put the money inside. I just wanted to end the whole game. If you still hadn't figured out the clues, I was going to tell you."

"But what happened to the money?"

"Someone else took it."

"Who?"

"I can't tell you, Nutty. Just take the money I put in your locker, and we'll call it square. Your dad won't have to pay anything, and the whole thing is over."

"But it isn't, Bilbo. There's still someone who knows how to get in my locker—besides you."

"No there isn't. You don't have to worry about that."

Nutty stared at Bilbo. He couldn't just let things end this way."

"Bilbo," William said, "this afternoon I put a lot of pressure on you. I wanted you to explain yourself. Why didn't you do it?"

Bilbo was looking toward the school again. He seemed nervous. "I knew you were on to me, but Nutty wasn't. I thought I would put the money back, and then talk to you—and get you not to tell anyone else."

"I see. I thought it was something of that sort. Last night you were actually trying to put the money back, weren't you? I saw you take something from your pocket."

Bilbo nodded, but Nutty said, "What's this?"

William said to Nutty, "Remember, I told you I thought I saw the thief last night?"

"Yes."

"Bilbo tried to get to your locker during that time that Skinner chased you down the hall. But Skinner turned back too soon, and he didn't get time."

"But remember," Bilbo said, "by then it was my own money I was trying to put in the locker. The other money was already stolen."

"And now you've got to tell us who stole it," Nutty said.

"I can't. I'm sorry, but I just can't." Bilbo got up.

"What are you afraid of?" William said.

Bilbo looked toward the school, not at William. "I'm not afraid of anything, not in the way you think." He started to walk away, but then he stopped and looked back. "William, how did you know I would come back this afternoon?"

"I forced you into a corner. You had to do something. I was almost sure you were trying to return the money. Right after school, once kids are gone, is the easiest time. I didn't think you would want to do it over the weekend, or on Monday morning."

"I thought about just bringing it to you," Bilbo said. "But then Nutty would have wanted an explanation."

"Yes, that occurred to me, too."

"You think of everything, William. Do you know who the real thief is?"

"I believe I do. Some of the last pieces in the puzzle have fallen into place now."

"Don't do anything about it, all right? Let's just leave things as they are. You could cause some real problems if you try to push this thing any further."

"But he has to," Nutty said. And now Nutty stood up. "Come on, Bilbo. We can't leave things the way they are."

Bilbo just looked at Nutty for a few seconds. And finally he said, "Listen, Nutty, I've said all I can say. It will be a lot better for *you* if you leave things alone at this point." Then he walked away.

Chapter XV

The Stinger

Nutty watched Bilbo for a few seconds, then turned to William, who was seated on the grass. "What do we do now?" he said. "Do you really have the last pieces of the puzzle?"

"Well, there's still a piece or two I don't have." He hesitated and looked thoughtful. It was a warm day for November. All the same, the afternoon air was getting cool. After a minute or so, William stood up and hiked his coat collar up around the back of his neck. "A couple of days ago, I knew something had changed," he said, and he still seemed to be running ideas through his head. "I suspected Bilbo after we got the second clue; but on the day after the double clue and the wiped-away chemical, his whole manner changed. I didn't know what had happened, but I could tell that something had. Bilbo almost seemed sick. The next morning you fellows had your conversation with Hobble and Fowler, and Fowler had said something rather strange. Orlando said Fowler asked where Bilbo was and whether he was feeling sick."

"He was just mouthing off about us always being together. He always does that."

"Yes, I understand that. All the same, he didn't say, 'Is he sick today?' He said, 'Is he feeling sick?' And that same evening, when we ran into those two, Fowler asked Bilbo the same thing, using those same words. It struck me at the time that he knew something, that he understood why Bilbo had changed on that particular day. It was one of those things I merely filed away, to consider as we went along."

"I know what you're talking about. I could tell those guys knew something, too. And I think they said something to Jerry Robinson. But I don't think that's enough to prove anything, at least not to some-one like Dr. Dunlop."

"I know. That's true, Nutty. But it fits some other things that are worth pursuing. Come on, I think we better make our move now, while we still have a chance." And away went William, walking straight toward the school.

"Where are you going?" Nutty kept asking, but William just kept walking, on in through the back door of the school.

"Just come with me," William said. "And don't say anything. Just let me handle everything. If I say some things that aren't exactly accurate, don't correct me. Just sit tight."

"Say things where? Who are you going to talk to?"

William didn't reply, just kept marching on—straight to Dr. Dunlop's open door. "Excuse me, sir," he said, "may I have a word with you?"

"Listen, Bilks, I told you not to—"

"I know, sir. But I'm here to tell you who the thief is. I thought you wouldn't mind knowing that."

"Come in. I do want to hear your opinion about that. But if you think—"

"Excellent," William said. "I think we'll have this all cleared up in no time." William walked in and sat down, and Nutty followed. "Could you please call Rod Fowler, Jim Hobble, and Bilbo—or I mean, Charley Blackhurst. And could you have them all come over here?"

"Are you accusing those three of taking the money?"

"I didn't say that. But I'm sure they can clear things up for us."

"Listen, I'm not going to call people here without any good reason for doing so."

"All right. Thanks anyway." William got up and walked toward the door. Nutty stood up too.

But Dunlop stood, himself, at that point. "Wait a minute," he said. And then he looked across his big desk and seemed rather baffled. "Well, all right. I'll call them. I do want this cleared up. But Bilks, I'm not putting up with your dealings any more after this."

"I would hope this would be the end of my . . . ah . . . dealings, sir."

Dunlop made the calls. As it turned out, Fowler was at Hobble's house, and the two were able to get back to the school rather quickly. But Bilbo had not yet arrived home, and Dunlop had to leave a message for him to return as quickly as he could.

A painfully awkward—and silent—six or seven minutes went by before Hobble and Fowler arrived. Until they did, William refused to discuss the case at all.

"Come in and sit down, boys," Dunlop said. Fowler and Hobble looked scared, especially when they came inside and took a look at William and Nutty sitting there. But Nutty had no idea what was going on. William seemed to be going way out on a limb this time.

"I believe, sir," William said, "that we can start without Bilbo."

"Then start."

"Thank you, sir." William got up and moved his chair forward; then he turned it, so he was looking

134

straight at Hobble and Fowler when he sat down again. "Now, fellows, as you know, you are in possession of a large sum of money that was taken from Nutty's locker. It was money for needy children, and you two stole it."

Both boys looked stunned. Hobble just shook his head, but Fowler turned very red and blurted out, "Oh no, we didn't. We didn't steal any money."

"Well, now, that's very interesting. Bilbo Blackhurst says that you stole the Christmas Fund, something close to two hundred dollars."

Hobble simply said, "No we didn't," and kept repeating it; but Fowler immediately said, "Two hundred dollars? He's lying."

"He is?"

"Yeah, he is."

"How do you know that?"

Fowler was about to say something when Hobble jumped in. "Because we didn't do it. That's why."

"Well, all right. Bilbo will be here in just a few minutes. We'll let him tell his side of the story, and then you can reply to it." William sat back comfortably in his chair, folded his arms across his chest, and turned to Dr. Dunlop. "It's been unseasonably warm this fall, hasn't it?"

Dunlop just stared at William. Then he shook his head as if to say, "I don't believe this."

But Nutty was now watching Hobble and Fowler. They were looking very uncomfortable, especially Fowler. It was not thirty seconds before he said, "Bilbo's the one who took the money."

Hobble cringed; then he looked over at Fowler and gave him a little shake of the head. But Nutty could see that Hobble's hands were shaking.

"Now that's very interesting you should say that," William said. "Could you tell me how you know that? I'm sure, when he gets here, he'll be interested to know that you said so."

"Look, I know what he'll say," Fowler said. "But he's lying. We even have proof that—"

"No," Hobble said, and he gave Fowler a quick jab with his elbow.

"What's this?" Dr. Dunlop said. "You say you have proof?"

"Dr. Dunlop, we didn't do it," Hobble said. "We didn't break into Nutty's locker, and that's the truth."

"But you say that Charles Blackhurst did?"

Hobble looked down. "I don't know about that," he mumbled.

"Well, let's see," William said. "I suspect Jim is telling the truth about the locker, Dr. Dunlop. I really doubt that either one of these young men has the intelligence to memorize a three-digit lock combination. I think mugging would be more in their line."

"Shut your mouth," Fowler said.

But Hobble gave him another elbow, and again he began his denials. "We didn't take it. That's all we're saying."

"Listen, Bilks," Dr. Dunlop said. "I don't understand what you're up to here. If you have anything to back up your opinion, say it; otherwise, let's end this right now."

"But can't you see how guilty they are? They're both about to go to pieces."

"Anyone would get nervous with someone making accusations like that. I don't see that you have proved anything. Now if these boys want to explain why they think the Blackhurst boy is the guilty one, I would like to hear that. If not, this whole thing has gone far enough."

Nutty knew they were losing now. He had little doubt that Fowler and Hobble were the thieves, but he knew that William's attempt to rattle them and get them to say something had failed. All the same, William looked as confident as ever.

"Dr. Dunlop," William said. "Let's just wait a few more minutes. Bilbo will be here, and he'll be able to clear everything up."

"But he may have gone somewhere. I'm not going to have these boys sit here any longer while you—"

"But sir, didn't you see Fowler's reaction when

I accused him of stealing two hundred dollars. He came very close to correcting me and telling me it was only eighty. Hobble stopped him just in time. Didn't you see that?"

Dunlop leaned back in his chair. "That may or may not be the case. But it's hardly enough to—"

But at that moment Bilbo stepped up to the door. "Ah, Bilbo," William said. "You are just in time."

Bilbo stepped in and looked around the room. The blood drained from his face. "William, I told you—"

"I know what you told me, Bilbo. You told me that these two young men took the eighty dollars. And that they then hung a threat over your head if you told on them. I'm not sure what they were going to do to you, but—"

"William, I didn't say any such thing. I don't know what you're talking about."

"Oh, for heaven's sake," Dunlop said, and he stood up. "All right, this is the end of this. Bilks, I never want to see your face in this school again. You have done nothing but—"

"But catch the thief, sir. It was Bilbo all along. Nutty is my witness. Bilbo admitted the whole thing this afternoon. He took the money and left marks on Nutty's locker as clues, all to try to outwit me. And he broke into the locker several times. Isn't that true, Nutty?"

Nutty was speechless. "Not exactly," he finally said. "I mean, he just did it to teach me a lesson. He wasn't going to keep the money."

Dunlop was bewildered and confused. "Charles, is there any truth to all this?"

Bilbo took a long breath. "Yes," he said. "But I didn't end up with the money. Those two did." He nodded his head toward Hobble and Fowler.

Fowler stood up. "I knew he would say that, but we have proof who it really was. Bilbo and Nutty did it themselves."

Hobble just sat there, looking down. He seemed to know that they had lost.

"Stole it *themselves*?" Dunlop said. "Frederick was in on it?"

"Yeah. And we have a note that proves it. Bilbo wrote it. It says that he and Nutty kept the money themselves and just made up the story that it was stolen."

William began to chuckle; Nutty began to choke; Bilbo began to hang his head; and all the while Dunlop was looking about as though someone had just scared up a flock of crows in his office.

"All right. The case is solved," William said. "I now have the last piece to the puzzle."

Chapter XVI

Stung

Everyone was sitting down now, except for William. He was standing in the middle of the room, holding the lapels of his coat and pacing back and forth. He looked like a big-city lawyer, addressing the jury.

"You see, sir," William said, "I have been bluffing to some degree. I was trying to get that final piece of the puzzle, and now I have it."

"We didn't do it," Fowler mumbled. "It was Nutty and Bilbo." But he didn't sound very convincing, not even very forceful; and Hobble was just looking at the floor.

"Here's what happened," William went on, ignoring Fowler. "Bilbo did something unwise, but not ill-intended. He took some money from Nutty's locker, always with the plan to return it. I'll explain the motivations in more detail later, but for now let's simply say that it was primarily a joke."

"A joke?" Dunlop said, and he seemed rather doubtful.

But William simply nodded and said, "Yes, primarily a joke. And then something about like this happened: we purposely dropped a hint to Hobble and Fowler here. We let them think that something valuable was still in Nutty's locker. At the time, we suspected them of the first theft. I think they went to the locker, probably not too long after school, and found Bilbo already there. He was in the act of returning the money. But these two scoundrels saw an opportunity to take the money for themselves. They did so, and they blackmailed Bilbo not to say anything." William strode back across the room and faced Bilbo. "Now, is that about the way it happened?"

"Sort of," Bilbo said. He looked over at Dunlop. "They said they were going to turn me in, so I tried to explain that I wasn't *stealing* money but putting it back. I told them why I had taken it—mainly to teach Nutty a lesson. But that gave them a better idea."

"He's lying," Fowler said. "We have a note that proves it."

William turned around. "Just hold on for now.

141

You'll have your chance." And then, turning back to Bilbo, "What was this 'better idea'?"

"They told me to give them the money. Hobble said that if Nutty didn't get the money back and got blamed for losing it, maybe the Student Council would vote to have him removed from office."

Dunlop looked over at Hobble, but Hobble never looked up.

"He's lying," Fowler said.

"I told them I was going to head straight for the office and tell you what was going on. But they said they would tell you that they had caught me bringing the money back." Bilbo shook his head. "I was in a real mess. I knew how that would look. So I just told them to go ahead and take the money. And what I was thinking was that I would pay back the money myself. That seemed better than having Nutty kicked out of office and me in all kinds of trouble for being a thief."

"They seemed, then, to have all the cards," William said. "Why was it that you agreed to write a note, and what did the note say?"

"Well, I think Hobble got worried that I would just wait until they walked away and then go straight to the office. I guess he was worried that Dr. Dunlop would believe me if I told him everything. So Hobble got the idea to have me write a note that said Nutty and I had stolen the money ourselves. It was addressed to Dr. Dunlop. They had me say I had a guilty conscience and wanted to admit the truth."

"And they would send this in if you tried to inform on them?"

"Yes."

"That's a dirty lie," Fowler said.

William turned around. "Then why do *you* have the note?"

"Because . . . because . . ." Fowler was sinking fast. Hobble had understood long before. "Because we found it," Fowler said, very weakly.

"Jim, what do you have to say?" Dr. Dunlop said.

Hobble didn't look up. He just said, "Most of it was Rod's idea."

Fowler almost dropped out of his seat. And then he spun toward Hobble. "What are you talking about? I—"

"That's enough," Dr. Dunlop said.

There were several seconds of silence, and then Fowler glared at William. "Well, you don't have to think you're so smart. We didn't get any clues from you. We just happened to walk out of the boys' room when Bilbo was putting the money in the locker."

"Nicely put," William said. "I *did* overestimate you."

Dunlop had many more questions after that. Eventually the whole story was clear, in detail. And Dunlop was not really pleased with anyone. He gave Nutty and Bilbo a good dressing down about the way they had handled things. Bilbo never should have started anything like that, and Nutty should have come straight to the office.

"And as for you, Bilks," Dr. Dunlop said. "You think you've solved all our problems, but I don't like one thing about the way you have handled these matters—breaking into the school, accusing people, deceiving almost everyone. I want you to stay at your own school and let us solve our own problems."

"I'll be happy to do just that," William said. "But all in all, I think things have turned out rather well. We have learned the truth. The money will be returned, I assume. Bilbo has learned an important lesson. And after all is said and done, Nutty learned some of the things Bilbo wanted him to learn."

Dunlop went off on another tirade about William's methods, but Nutty wasn't listening. He wasn't sure at all that he had learned any lessons, but he really did want to improve the way he was operating as president.

"Well, now, you three boys can leave," Dunlop was saying. "I can assure you that I'll be talking to your parents and that punishment of some sort will be in order." He then told Hobble and Fowler to sit where they were, that he was calling in their parents immediately.

William thanked Dr. Dunlop and was leaving, with Bilbo right behind him, when Nutty stopped and said, "Dr. Dunlop, while I have the chance, I wanted to ask whether you looked at those menus yet?"

Dunlop gave him a long, cold stare. He obviously couldn't believe what he had heard. Finally he said, "No—I have not. We'll have to discuss that some other time."

"How about Monday?"

"I have other matters to attend to right now, as you well know."

"But you could look at them over the weekend."

Dunlop took his glasses off, rubbed his eyes, and then said, "We'll see. In any case, I'll get to them soon."

"All right, I'll check with you early next week." Dunlop's eyes rolled, but Nutty paid no attention. He went on outside.

Bilbo was looking at Nutty, shaking his head in disbelief. "What are you trying to do, Nutty?"

"Improve the food around here," Nutty said, grinning. "I gotta start being a *real* president."

William chuckled and slapped him on the back.

"That's good, Nutty," he said. "But what, after all, *is* a real president? Things that seem real—as we have learned—are not always what we think them to be. Masterminds seem to be thieves, and thieves turn out not to be masterminds at all."

"Yeah, and guys who don't believe in telling lies sometimes tell plenty of them."

"Well, now, Nutty, I wouldn't say that I ever exactly lied. I sometimes—"

"Never mind, William. I don't want to run through this whole thing again. I'm sticking to the simple stuff from now on."

"Fine. That may be just as well. In fact, let me make a suggestion. Why don't you go to your locker and get out the eighty dollars that belongs to the Christmas Fund. I believe you left it there again."